EDMUND+OCTAVIA

The Dulcie Chambers Museum Mysteries

by Kerry J Charles

LAST OF THE VINTAGE

A Dulcie Chambers Museum Mystery

Kerry J Charles

EDMUND+OCTAVIA

This book is a work of fiction. Names, characters, places, and
incidents either are products of the author's imagination or are
used fictitiously. Any resemblance to actual events or locales or
persons, living or dead, is entirely coincidental.

Cover Image: *A Young Man Drinking*, 1700-1750, artist unknown,
in the style of Bartolomé Esteban Murillo. This image is in the
public domain.

ISBN: 0989457680
ISBN-13: 978-0-9894576-8-2

Edmund+Octavia Publishing, Falmouth, Maine, USA

For Stan

CONTENTS

Have no fear of perfection,
you'll never reach it.
~ Salvador Dali

CHAPTER ONE

The waves crashed against the nearby rocks, dangerously close to the tiny cottage. The entire house shook again and again with an ominous predictability. In the seven years of Hazel's entire existence living on the island, she had never heard waves like these before.

She had wanted to go outside to see them, but her mother wouldn't let her. "No," her mother had said firmly. "Besides, there's no moon. You can't see anything, anyway."

This was true. Thick black clouds had rolled in during the afternoon and the winds howled along with them, all through the night. The first hint of light now crept above the horizon, and Hazel couldn't hold back any longer. She slowly eased herself out of the bed, hoping that her mother wouldn't wake up just yet.

Her mother had been awake for nearly the entire night. She had shielded the light of the paraffin lamp so that it wouldn't shine directly toward the bed. She sat at the table with her book, pretending to read. Hazel knew that she wasn't. Her mother hadn't turned a single page.

Hazel normally slept in the loft upstairs, except during storms. Then she slept in the bigger bed downstairs, at her mother's insistence. All that her mother could picture was the roof coming off the house or a tall pine tree falling through it.

Hazel crept toward the door and opened it. She slipped outside. The air was warm and wet, strange for October. She could feel the crash of the surf through the stone step beneath her bare feet. From her vantage point, she could easily see the waves. They were massive, at least four or five times taller than she was. A shiver ran down her spine.

She followed the swells backward, out toward the open ocean. Something strange caught her eye farther away. It looked like the mast of a ship, except sideways. She squinted in the early dawn light. The object disappeared, then reappeared with each swell. She thought she could see a white sail fluttering around it.

The waves followed the usual routine of several comparatively smaller swells followed by one or two much larger ones. As she watched, a bigger wave hit the object and it disappeared. It bobbed back up again only to be hit by another large wave. She lost sight of the object again and stood watching, waiting for it to reappear. It never did.

Hazel stood on the front step for several more minutes wondering what she had just seen. Finally she convinced herself that it was simply a floating log with seagulls flying around it. She had seen debris like that in the water before, and gulls circled anything bobbing around, always looking for an easy meal. She nodded once, happy with her conclusion, yawned, then tiptoed back inside. She slid into bed again beside her mother and fell back asleep.

ॐ

Dulcie rummaged through the closet and found her down vest. She slipped into it, zipped it all the way up, then put her winter coat on over it. She was already wearing heavy boots. The coat came down below her knees, almost reaching the tops of the boots. Next she pulled on a knit hat, flipped her hood up over it, then wrapped a scarf around her neck several times until it covered the entire lower half of her face. She looked in the mirror and laughed. Only her eyes and her hands were visible. She made sure that her bag was securely closed, then put on heavy gloves. Slinging the bag over one arm she turned to open the door. She couldn't grip the knob so she had to take off one glove, grab the knob again, open the door, then put the glove back on. "And we have two more months of this?" she said out loud.

She stepped outside, closing the door firmly behind her, making sure that it was locked. The first breath that she inhaled made her gasp. Her scarf had slipped down, and the frigid air hit her lungs like a hammer. They now felt like Styrofoam. Her nose seemed to be frozen from the inside as well. She shoved the scarf up with her gloved hand and began to trudge down the street.

Dulcie hadn't even attempted to start her vehicle that morning. The old Jeep Wrangler that she loved had seen better days. She knew it would be an exercise in futility to listen to the starter grind over and over again with absolutely no hope of it kicking the engine into action. All it would do was wear down the battery.

She scuffled down the street, walking quickly to stay warm. Two below, the thermometer had read. It didn't matter. Once you reach a certain state of coldness it all feels the same. Normally the walk took ten minutes. Today it was much quicker since she nearly jogged the entire distance.

Oddly, there hadn't been much snow. Decembers were always iffy in terms of snowfall. Sometimes there was a white Christmas, sometimes not. January typically brought plenty of storms, but this year seemed to be an exception. So far, there were only dustings of an inch or two. It appeared that the weather gods were making up for that by bringing in the subzero temperatures instead.

When she reached the museum, she glanced out across the harbor. It looked nearly frozen in again. It was a strange sight, a long, gray, very flat surface that suddenly connected two land masses which had been long separated by water. It wouldn't last, however. The ice breaker would come through it again, chopping a path for boats to use as they came and went. There were always boats in the harbor. Granted, far fewer during the winter months, but some still braved the cold. It was Maine after all. A true Yankee couldn't let a little thing like below zero temperatures stop the general industry.

Dulcie unlocked the museum door with some difficulty as she did not want to take off her gloves. She pushed it open and felt a blast of heat hit her. Now she pulled off her gloves, pressed the security code on the keypad, and heard the inner door lock click. She leaned against the heavy glass door and went inside.

In her office it took a good ten minutes to slide off all of her outer layers, change into her shoes, fix her hair, and make sure she was somewhat presentable. Her assistant, Rachel, tapped on the doorframe and popped her head in. "Enjoy the stroll in this morning?" she quipped.

"Holy cow!" Dulcie replied. "If that doesn't wake me up, nothing will!"

Rachel giggled "How about some coffee? I was just getting some. Then we can go over the setup for the new exhibit."

"Have I ever told you that you're an angel?" Dulcie said.

"I'm just a morning person," Rachel laughed. "Be right back." She scooted out of the room.

"And I am, most decidedly, not," Dulcie muttered to herself. She took her laptop out of her bag and flipped it open on her desk. First she glanced through her calendar, then quickly flicked through email, pausing to read a few messages, but deleting most. Somehow the spam filter never seemed to catch everything. She was just about to close the computer when a familiar name popped up.

"Huh!" Dulcie exclaimed, sitting back in her chair.

"Huh, what?" asked Rachel, walking back in with coffee and her own laptop under her arm.

"Huh!" Dulcie said again, then looked up at her assistant. "It seems that my old boyfriend from Oxford is coming to town. He wants to have lunch with me."

"Oooohhhhh!" Rachel hooted. "And how will the new beau handle that, I wonder?"

"With poise and decorum, I'm sure. Things have been decidedly over for a long time with Mr. Brendan MacArthur," Dulcie replied.

She and Portland police detective Nicholas Black had recently begun dating. They had agreed go slowly. Nick had initiated the relationship, or at least inadvertently revealed his feelings for her, before ending a previous attachment. It didn't exactly make him appear to be the most trustworthy person in Dulcie's eyes. She knew that there had been

6

circumstances to explain the entire situation, and everyone else seemed to think that she was making far too much of it, but still. She had always trusted her instincts, and they were always right. Well, they were right most of the time.

Rachel was still talking. "I'm sorry, I wasn't listening. What did you just say?" Dulcie asked.

Rachel snickered. "You're sure things are over? You looked pretty lost just then!" She put up her hand to stop Dulcie's retort. "Okay, okay! Yes, I'm sure they are. But what's up? What brings him here?"

"I don't know," Dulcie said. "He says he's been working on a project and would love to talk with me about it."

"An art project?" Rachel replied.

"I can't imagine it would be. Brendan was never really interested in art. It was one of the many things that we did not have in common. He became an archaeologist, but I don't think it was to learn about antiquities necessarily. The thrill of the hunt seemed far more interesting to him. Once he'd located a site, he seemed less interested and mostly left it up to others to do the excavation. I remember that when we parted ways, he had begun to look for shipwrecks. Last I heard he'd been all over the world with a diving crew. They actually found a few minor wrecks I think."

"Wow, that's pretty exciting," said Rachel. "But really expensive I'd think. How'd he get the money, I wonder? Grants? University funds?" Rachel could always be counted on to bring practicality into any conversation.

Dulcie smiled. "That was another thing about Brendan. He was never lacking in funds. He came from money, family money. He could pretty much do whatever he wanted."

"Must be nice," Rachel mused. "So what did you two have in common?"

Dulcie took a deep breath. What they did have in common was something nearly as ancient as mankind. Something that, at its peak of perfection, was almost indescribable. They had even travelled around Europe hoping to find the hidden and elusive flawless vintage.

"Wine," Dulcie said simply. "What we had in common was wine."

ର

Detective Nicholas Black looked up from his desk as a shadow loomed over him. "Hey! You're back!" he grinned.

"That I am," answered detective Adam Johnson. He lumbered around his partner and sat down in his battered chair behind the desk facing Nick's.

"And looking very svelte, might I add!" Nick exclaimed.

"Hey, no comments from the peanut gallery!" Johnson growled. "I won that bet fair and square. I just chose to go to the weight loss center. Figured I could learn a thing or two."

Johnson had spent an agonizing month trying to lose weight after making a bet with his wife. If she won, he would go to a weight loss center for a week. If he won, he would go to the Boston Red Sox baseball spring training camp in Florida and see them play, "While eating all the sausages I want!" he never failed to mention.

"You won but you still went to the spa? Are you crazy?" Nick was surprised.

"Well, here's how it went down. I lost the ten pounds, so I won the bet. But when I went back to the doctor, he said I was still about ten pounds into the 'obese' category. If I lost another ten, I'd merely be in the 'overweight' category. I can live with overweight, but obese just made it sound gross."

"Literally," said Nick. He eyed his partner. "Ya know, now that you mention it, you have lost some weight. Did it help with the snoring?"

Adam Johnson's wife, Maria, had complained bitterly about his snoring, prompting the initial visit to the doctor. He had objected of course, but was summarily overruled by his wife. Adam had expected to hear that the snoring was normal and nothing could be done. After all, everyone in Johnson's entire family snored like a freight train. But the doctor said that it was because Johnson was overweight, or rather, 'obese' as he had put it. Thinking about it, Johnson realized that pretty much all of his family could fall into that category too. They were a group of hearty eaters. When Maria heard this, she instigated the bet.

"Maria says it has, but how do I know? I mean, I'm asleep, right?"

"Good point," Nick chuckled. "So no Sox games at spring training camp?"

Johnson stared at him for a moment. "Are you joking? Of course I'm still doing that! I mean, I won the bet!"

"So I'll have to learn to live without you for another week in April," said Nick. "How will I ever face it?"

Johnson threw a crumpled wad of paper at his partner. "Oops. Sorry. Aiming for the trash can."

Nick grabbed it off the floor and flicked it across the room, into the trash. "Yeah, it's over there numbskull."

Johnson ignored him. "So what did I miss?" he asked.

Nick rolled his eyes. "A whole lotta nuthin," he answered. "Seriously, not a single case. I've resorted to going back through the cold files. Care to hear about any of them?"

"If I say 'No' will it make any difference?" Johnson asked.

"Probably not," Nick said. "But job security, after all. Have to stay busy."

"Let's stay busy and go get a coffee," Johnson suggested.

"Uh, you do realized it's like a hundred below out?" Nick replied.

"Yeah, but you burn more calories in the cold! See, I learned that at fat camp!"

"I don't think I need to burn more calories right now," Nick said.

"Johnson stood up and started putting on the coat he'd slung over the back of his chair. "Yeah, you think that now, but you just wait another ten years. The ol' metabolism slows down and you start packing on the pounds before you know it. Best to get into good habits as early as you can!"

"I'm not sure I like the new and improved Johnson," grumbled Nick.

"Yes you do! Of course you do! Now get your lazy butt out of that seat and c'mon." He was already heading toward the door, pulling on a black knit hat that made him look unnervingly like a bank robber.

Nick shook his head, sighed and, grabbing his own coat, followed Johnson out the door.

♋

Brendan MacArthur stood in the tiny cabin of the fishing boat he had rented and peeled off his dry suit. One other crew member was doing the same beside him. The other two were on the bridge, steering the vessel back into Portland harbor.

Earlier in the fall Brendan had carried out methodical research to locate a clipper ship that had gone missing in 1869. He had even located the diary of a woman who, as a little girl, had lived on one of the farthest islands in Casco Bay. In one passage she recalled, "either something real or something I dreamt that looked quite like the mast of a ship with tattered sails amongst huge crashing surf." Brendan knew that people who lived by the ocean had a far different definition of 'huge crashing surf' than those who did not. If this girl said the waves were huge, then they must have been monsters.

Brendan was thorough. He had found as much information as he could on the woman. He also checked weather records for 1869. There was one major culprit that had slammed into Maine's coast: the Saxby Gale. It had taken place in October. The woman's diary recalled that the event had happened in the fall of that year. He carefully pieced together the facts which led him to one conclusion: there was a 19th century shipwreck off the tip of Cliff Island at a location known as Johns Ledge.

Why hadn't anyone else found it? Maybe the woman had dreamt the whole thing as a little girl. Maybe it wasn't really there. Maybe it had broken up to the extent that there was nothing left. Maybe it was covered with so much debris and seaweed that nobody recognized it as a ship.

Or maybe no one had bothered to look.

Brendan had been very excited, but he had to contain every ounce of it. He was part archaeologist, part treasure hunter. He knew from experience that only extremely trustworthy people could be told about this possibility. And given that Johns Ledge was relatively close to Cliff Island, now inhabited by quite a few people, he didn't want to be observed there either.

He called together his closest group of colleagues. They couldn't exactly be called friends, but they had at least two common interests: scuba diving and treasure hunting. They were all too willing to look at the site.

The four men had planned two exploratory dives, one in September and one in October. Brandan was careful to rent a different boat each time. To the average onlooker, the men would appear to be just another group of recreational divers.

Ironically, it was during the October dive that they had found it, nestled into the ledge about 24 feet down. They had located it at the end of the dive and had little air left. They stayed down as long as they could, using up every last ounce in their tanks.

As a trained archaeologist, Brendan knew that he probably would be able to oversee the excavation. The site would have to be made known to the state. But not quite yet. Brendan had to think about his next move. He had to plan carefully. He was very good at that.

His fellow divers were not as excited about the site. An initial inspection showed them that it really didn't contain anything valuable. The ship had hauled goods for trade that would have brought in a very high profit at the time, but were worth little now.

Brendan decided that one more dive was needed. A winter dive. It was dangerous at that time of year, but Cliff Island had far fewer people on it in the winter. All of the seasonal cottages would be closed up tight. He and his crew could get down to the wreck and bring up a few things 'off the record.' Then he would officially announce the find, register it, and start the actual 'boring archaeology bit' as he called it.

They had pulled up a couple of crates with porcelain dishes when Brendan found something which was potentially of great value that the others had missed. He had located a crate of bottles and they appeared to be full of wine. He had replaced the bottle that he had pulled out quickly. No one else had seen them. The others would find out eventually, but he wanted to learn as much as he could before they did. It would give him an advantage, and Brendan certainly knew how to make good use of an advantage.

With his dry suit off and jeans, heavy socks, boots, sweater, jacket… all of the other layers needed to brave the freezing air now on, Brendan turned to his crewmate. "So, Alan looks like not much."

"Yeah," Alan replied. "Some of the cargo was packed well though. Could be unbroken porcelain dishes and such. Collectors like that stuff. Could get some bucks for that."

Technically, anything as old as this wreck found in coastal waters belonged to the government. But Brendan and his colleagues had to make a living. They helped themselves to a few things first before announcing any new find. When it was time to sell the items, "I found it in grandma's attic," was always an excellent provenance.

Brendan was careful to be sure that the pieces they helped themselves to were more commonplace; nothing of great value or significance could be taken outright. It wasn't that he cared about their place in history, he just didn't want to get caught.

"True. Worth bringing those few crates up I suppose." Brendan said. "I'll have to set up a grid and record some things too, once we're done getting our share. Have to keep the authorities happy." As soon as he made the wreck known, funding would come in to analyze it. He'd never had much of a problem with that. It was bread and butter money for him and his colleagues. Enough to pay the regular bills, but not much extra.

The archaeological part was tedious work. He hoped that a PhD candidate would step forward to take on the project. They almost always did. Then Brendan could move on to the next search.

"What about that wine?"

Brendan froze, then frowned. He hadn't realized that Alan had seen it. "Must have turned by now. Can't keep even the best of that stuff for more than half a century or so, I think," Brendan lied. "That wine has to be at least 150 years old down there." He shrugged. "The bottles themselves might have some value. Worth bringing up I guess." He motioned toward the boat's bridge overhead. "You coming up?" he asked, trying to change the subject as quickly as possible. It worked.

"Nah," Alan responded. "Too crowded up there. I think I'll just take a short nap. We've got probably half an hour or so before we're back in, yeah?" He didn't wait for an answer. He was already adjusting the life preservers to create a reasonably comfortable bed.

Brendan chuckled to himself. Alan always had been the lazy one.

The longer you look at an object,
the more abstract it becomes,
and, ironically, the more real.
~ Lucian Freud

CHAPTER TWO

"This weather girl is really good at delivering the forecast, but she's terrible at the banter with the news desk guy," Dulcie announced as she switched off the television. Nick had just rounded the corner into the kitchen of her townhouse to put the Chinese take-out leftovers in the fridge.

He poked his head back around the corner. "Weather *girl?* "

"Oh. Right. I mean Weather Woman. Weather Lady. What the heck do I call her? Weather Forecaster? Yeah, I'll stick with that," Dulcie replied.

Nick came back into the room shaking his head. "you, of all people..." he trailed off.

"I know! You're right! But some labels just stick, unfortunately!"

"I know what you mean," Nick said, walking over to the window. He looked outside. January. In spite of the fact that it wasn't very late, it had been dark for a couple of hours already. He had never liked January.

He came back to the couch and sat down with Dulcie. "Finish this off?" he asked, gesturing toward the wine bottle.

"Why not," Dulcie smiled.

Nick carefully poured what was left in both of their glasses. "This is really good," he said.

"Life's too short for bad wine," Dulcie replied.

"Amen to that!" Nick laughed. They were silent for a moment. The pause wasn't awkward, but they were both aware of it.

Nick sat back and relaxed. "So tell me about this new exhibit."

Dulcie's face was instantly animated. "It's great! I'm loving it, and the timing couldn't be more perfect! It's a travelling exhibit, but we're the first museum to show it in the US, which is pretty fabulous. A coup for us! Plus we've added some pieces from our own collection."

"Okay, that's all great but what's the theme?"

Dulcie began to laugh. "It's called: The Little Ice Age: Winter in Europe from the 14th to 19th century."

"You're kidding! How long did you know about this?"

"The committee put the whole thing together over a year ago. I had no idea it would be so perfectly timed!"

"But could that work against you? I mean, it's freezing out. Do you think people really want to see pictures of more snow and ice?" Nick asked

Dulcie toyed with her glass for a moment. "I've thought about that, but I believe they would. Or at least, it's more relatable this time of year."

Nick nodded. "True." He sipped thoughtfully. "But educate me. I thought the last ice age was something like ten thousand years ago?"

"This wasn't really a true ice age, according to scientists anyway. But it was a time period when it was colder in the Northern Hemisphere. Most of the more famous paintings that show winter scenes were done during that period. Bruegel in the 16th century, Avercamp in the 17th, Raeburn in the 18th. The Thames froze over, parts of the Bosphorus were frozen, and the canals in the Netherlands of course were frozen. The Swedish army even used it to their advantage, marching across the frozen sea into Denmark and conquering part of the country. This is why I love art history. It isn't just a bunch of paintings and sculptures. It tells a story." Dulcie stopped, slightly embarrassed by her monologue.

Nick hid his smile. Dulcie was passionate about her work, and he loved that about her. He loved pretty much everything about her. He put down his now empty glass on the coffee table in front of him. "Well then, I can't wait to see the whole exhibit. Do you have anyone special coming to town for it? You have visiting artists or professors sometimes, right?"

Dulcie's mood shifted instantly. She had been excited, animated, talking about the new exhibit with Nick. Now she remembered Brendan. She had to tell Nick about him. Dulcie sighed. Now was as good a time as any.

"Well, no, nobody connected with the exhibit anyway. But Nick, there is someone coming to town who wants to have lunch with me to talk about a project. He's an archaeologist, actually mostly an underwater archaeologist now. He also happens to be an old boyfriend from my Oxford days."

Nick looked at the floor. "Ah. I see."

"He and I are long over. There's nothing between us at all. I haven't even heard from him for a couple of years. He just got in touch out of the blue. And I think he just wants to have lunch as more of a business meeting and not a social kind of thing…."

"Dulcie, it's fine. I know you have a past. God knows I have one." It had been the major problem that had divided them until recently, the reason why Dulcie had been hesitant to get involved with Nick. "Of course I'm not thrilled that an old flame is in town. Who would be? But I trust you." He brushed away a wisp of dark hair from her cheek, his fingers grazing her soft skin.

Dulcie blushed instantly. Her glass was tilted so much that she was nearly spilling wine on the rug. She quickly held it upright, then put it down on the table with a decided clink. "I appreciate that," she said knowing she sounded stupid. "I just wanted you to know. From me. I mean, I'm sure my dumb brother would have blurted it out, so I figured I'd best be the one to say something." Dulcie knew she was babbling again. She took a deep breath. "I don't know what this project is about, but if it's interesting I'll let you know." For some reason she'd slipped into her businesslike voice.

Nick decided to spare her from making a complete fool of herself and changed the subject. "That sounds great. So when does your brother get back?"

Dulcie let out a long, slow breath. Nick's conversational maneuver was quite obvious, but she was grateful nonetheless. "This weekend. He won't be happy about the cold weather, either."

"A far cry from the Florida sunshine. Did he like the boat show?"

"He loved it! I think he went out with a different woman each night. That's my brother. He has a lot of wild oats to sow, evidently."

Nick laughed. "Some have more than others, yes. He'll settle down eventually."

Dulcie wasn't so sure, but that was all right. Dan was Dan. He made no pretense to be anything else but himself. And everyone liked him all the more for it. Except for a few women who had fallen for him prematurely and had their hearts broken. That was bound to happen, though.

"I have to check on his boat tomorrow during the five minutes of sunshine that we may or may not have, according to the Weather *Forecaster*." She enunciated the term.

"Very good!" Nick grinned. He glanced at his watch. "I should get going. I promised Johnson I'd stop by. He said it was to hand off some files on a cold case, but I think the real reason is that he wants me to say how great he looks in front of Maria."

Nick stood and walked toward the door. Dulcie followed him, handing him his jacket. "And does he? Did he lose a lot?"

Nick began to laugh. "Under normal circumstances, you might call it a lot. For him, it's more like a drop in the bucket. As he put it, 'I went from being obese to just plain overweight.' That pretty much sums it up."

"Oh my!" Dulcie grinned. "I will have to compliment him when I see him next, though. Hopefully all the positive feedback will keep him on the straight and narrow."

"Straight, maybe. Narrow is questionable," Nick replied. He leaned over, kissed her softly on the lips, and whispered, "See you soon!" Then he left, closing the door behind him.

Dulcie was glad he'd gone so quickly. A glance in the mirror beside the door was all she needed to prove that her cheeks were now bright red.

☙

"Jeremy, would you please remember to empty the damned spit cup and clean everything up? I've told you about a thousand times!" Samantha Sanders was not at all happy with her husband at the moment. Come to think of it, she hadn't really been happy with him for quite some time. This wine thing was really getting annoying.

Jeremy came into the dining room. The table was littered with wine glasses and bottles with varying levels of wine remaining in most of them. Samantha wheeled around, hands on hips, and glared at him. "I can handle seeing this mess. I know you need to keep practicing. It's just the damn spit thing is really disgusting!"

He took the spit cup into the kitchen, emptied it into the sink, rinsed it out, and put it in the dishwasher. She followed him with as many glasses as she could carry.

"Sorry, Sam. I know you're getting frustrated. The exam is only a month away. I'm nearly there. I'm really feeling good about my Alsatians now too!"

It was wine. Always wine, wine, wine! She was sick of it. "Can we talk about something else, please?" she asked, clearly annoyed.

"Like what? What do you want to talk about?" her husband replied.

"Like maybe my career? And our future? Not just yours?"

The whole wine thing had seemed so glamorous at first. Samantha had listened intently as Jeremy had talked about different regions and different vintages.

She had tried various wines and was learning to tell the difference between a Bordeaux and a Merlot. Whenever Jeremy's friends came over to quiz each other or practice tasting, she could carry on reasonably intelligent conversations with them about their common obsession. But it was rarely reciprocated. "I'm just the weather girl," she thought.

Samantha had always loved meteorology growing up. She'd learned all of the clouds and would watch their patterns intently, predicting what would happen the next day. It wasn't long before everyone started calling her "weather girl" because, by age 12, she could forecast, with uncanny accuracy, what the weather would be like the next day.

It wasn't just the clouds, either. As she grew older she would drive out into the countryside around Portland and stop the car. She would sit and watch how the birds were flying, what the squirrels were doing, subtle shifts in the breeze. Weather was intuitive for her. It was a part of her.

The TV job had been a bit of a fluke. She had never imagined herself delivering the evening forecast. In fact, she often had thought of those people as puppets who just read what the computers told them. They didn't actually *know* the weather, they just had a bit more advance information than everyone else.

During her senior year in college, where she had majored in meteorology of course, she was facing some large student loan debts. For most of the four years she had been dating the same person, a fellow meteorology student from a wealthy family. They had talked about a future together. Whenever she mentioned her student loans, he would tell her not to worry. They both planned to continue on through graduate school. He would then become a college professor, and she would find a research job. Their path was clear.

Samantha had not seen it coming. At their graduation she was about to line up for the diploma ceremony, finding her place in alphabetical order, when he had pulled her aside. "Look, Sam," he had said. "I know we've talked about a lot of things, but I really need a fresh start. We've had a lot of fun, and you're obviously great, but I just need to be on my own, you know?"

No, she did not know.

She remembered staring at him with her mouth open. She remembered closing it slowly. She remembered how cold his eyes had been as he stared back at her. She still felt sick whenever she recalled the scene.

Samantha had not replied. She had simply turned and walked away. She thought she heard him say, "Maybe we can get in touch sometime later on, in a few months?" She ignored him.

The rest of the day was a predictable blur. She got her diploma, thankfully without tripping on the stage. She smiled for all of the family photos. She pretended to eat at the celebratory dinner. A few people asked about her boyfriend, but she was able to brush off their questions with casual replies.

Later that night she went back to her dorm room to pack up all of her things. A picture of the two of them sat on the desk. She tried to ignore it. It seemed to mock her, so she tipped it over, barely touching it, so that it was face down on the wooden surface. She methodically packed her things in the boxes that her parents brought to the room, chatting with them, pretending to be happy. When they were done the picture was still on the desk. "Oh, don't forget this!" her mom had said, handing it to Samantha.

She put it on top of the box she was carrying and followed them out the door. When they passed a large trash can in the parking lot outside, Samantha quietly tossed the picture in. Done. Gone.

Samantha had been accepted to graduate school, the same one as her now ex-boyfriend, and had planned to begin in the fall. A week after graduation she contacted them to defer her admission for a year. She still wasn't sure what she would do. By now, her parents knew about the breakup.

Samantha's mother had seen the advertisement during the summer. A local TV station was looking for an on-air forecaster. "Sam, you'd be great at this!" her mother said. "You've always been our *weather girl* you know!" Not only did Samantha have the knowledge to do the job, she had one other qualifying characteristic that most women would kill for, but that Samantha found difficult to manage.

She was a bombshell.

Honey-blonde hair, large green eyes, a perfect hourglass figure, and an innate poise that, all combined, made innocent bystanders stop their conversations and simply watch her walk by. Samantha had never been comfortable with any of it. She did not like attention.

But she had those crushing student loans. So she applied for the job. And of course, she got it. Within a week, she was the most watched weather forecaster of all the networks. She knew why, and it wasn't because she was more accurate than anyone else, which of course she was. The only satisfaction that she got from it was that she hoped her stupid ex-boyfriend saw her and regretted breaking up with her. Probably not.

Samantha had made a promise to herself that she would stay on television for only one year to pay off her loans. Meanwhile, she would start graduate coursework at the nearby state university. Then she would transfer to one of the more well-known programs to begin the path toward a research position.

That had been three years ago. That same summer, she had met Jeremy. They went through a whirlwind romance and before she knew it, she was married. Samantha wouldn't allow herself to believe that it was a rebound relationship.

"Are you getting tired of the weather girl gig?" Jeremy asked, taking a few of the glasses from her.

Samantha's thoughts were jerked into the present. "Stop calling it that!" she spat out, then wished she hadn't. It wasn't so much that she disliked being called a weather girl, it was just that the entire 'gig' as Jeremy referred to it, was exactly the opposite of what she wanted to do with her life. "I'm sorry," she said. "I mean, it's just not the career I had dreamed of."

"But it's good pay while you're in school," Jeremy said. "And while I'm trying to get this master somm certification."

Back to that. Somehow every conversation went back to him and his master level certification as a sommelier. Samantha knew it was a big step in his career. The level was highly coveted, and few had reached it. It would open doors for him to work literally around the world. But did Samantha want to go through those doors with him?

"Yeah," she said while loading the dishwasher. "It's good pay." They were silent as they cleaned up the kitchen, then both went to their respective rooms to study. Jeremy had already forgotten the conversation. Samantha couldn't stop thinking about it.

ॐ

He walked slowly down the dark street, stumbling occasionally on the icy sidewalk. He'd forgotten his gloves, so his hands were shoved into this pockets to protect them from the freezing blasts of air that whistled between the buildings. Every few feet he slipped, and his hands would involuntarily come out of his pockets to balance him. He swore softly each time, replacing his hands in the comparative warmth the moment he'd regained his balance.

28

When he reached the corner he paused and looked up. Her window. He knew it was her window. He had seen her standing there, looking out, several times. Once he had thought she was looking directly back at him and restrained the urge to wave. Not now. Not yet.

Did this make him a stalker, the fact that he kept walking down the same street every evening, looking up toward the same window, hoping to see the same person? It wasn't like he waited outside her door and followed her. Still, what exactly was he doing?

They had been together for so long. He thought that he wanted to be free, to date other women, to have the options for his life open. That first summer had been fun, but as the days grew colder and he went off to graduate school, he found himself thinking about her. A lot.

He had buckled down, focused on his work, finished his masters degree. It had been a struggle. He knew he had to see her again. He had to talk to her. He had to get her back.

He moved to Maine and got a job teaching at the local community college. It wasn't the high-powered professorship that he had planned, but he didn't care now. He just wanted Samantha back.

It had come as a shock to turn on the television one night and see her, delivering the weather forecast. His days now revolved around the evening news. He even recorded her and watched her over and over, long into the evening.

Portland was a very small city, and it didn't take long for him to learn more about her. She was married. She had been for three years, since the summer after he had dumped her. "Didn't take her long," he thought, not realizing that his face had contorted into a sneer. Had he expected her to pine for him? Of course he had.

He wasn't sure what his next move would be. He had a vague idea of them 'bumping into' one another, but it seemed too obvious. Why would he be there, after all? Other than general family connections, he really had no reason to even be visiting Portland. He certainly had no reason to be living and working there.

He pushed the crosswalk signal and, while waiting for it to change, continued to stare up at the window. The light was on, but he couldn't see anyone. The traffic signal switched and he reluctantly continued across the street, back toward his own apartment.

Samantha stood behind the curtain. She had been watching him. She knew he was there. She had first seen him several weeks earlier. Her stomach had dropped that first time. She tried to convince herself that it wasn't him, but that was useless. She knew, without a doubt, that it was.

The next time she saw him, she made a point of standing in the window, in full view. For the entire time she stood there, willing herself not to look down at him, he stared up at her. Yes, it had to be him.

Samantha now found herself gripped by an unexplained fear. Every nerve in her body told her that something was wrong. He shouldn't be here. He should be long gone from her life by now. Why had he suddenly reappeared? What did he want? She tried to calm herself, to convince herself that any interest he had was benign. But she knew him. She knew his obsessive nature. He didn't give up on something if he wanted it. He was insidious, charming when necessary, forceful when required. Their relationship had been on his terms, always.

When she thought back, she was glad that it had ended. She just wished that she hadn't fallen into a marriage so quickly with someone new. She wished she had taken time for herself. But Samantha had always been affected by everyone else. She had grown to be incapable of standing up for herself, or even knowing who, exactly, she was.

Patrick Spratt trudged back to his small apartment, now shivering from the arctic air. He unwound the scarf from around his neck and scuffed off the bottoms of his boots on the front mat while removing his coat. Reaching down with cold hands, he took the boots off and padded into the living room where he switched on the TV. He went into the kitchen, opened a beer, and came back out. Without even looking at it, he picked up the remote and hit several buttons. Samantha's face appeared on the screen. The volume was off. He sat in silence, staring at her, drinking his beer, for nearly an hour.

One can have no smaller
or greater mastery
than mastery of oneself.
~ Leonardo da Vinci

CHAPTER THREE

Dulcie tried not to fidget. She held her coffee cup firmly in both hands, willing her body to relax. It was silly, really. Why should she be so nervous to see Brendan MacArthur again? What difference did it make? It had been several days since she'd received his message, but she still hadn't come to terms with a reunion on any level.

"Ah, there's my bonnie wee lassie!" a voice with a decided Scottish brogue chimed from behind her. She flinched and spilled the coffee. "And here I am scaring you to bits!" he added.

Dulcie gently lowered the cup, turned, and smiled. "Brendan, so good to see you," she said trying, and failing, to keep a more formal tone. "I was lost in thought," she added by way of an excuse, wiping up coffee from the table with a paper napkin. It was an effective means to avoid what would have been a bear hug from her former boyfriend.

He settled for sliding his arm around her waist and pulling her sideways toward him for a brief moment. She laughed awkwardly. He eased into the chair opposite her.

"So now that I've ruined your drink, I can buy you a proper one as any gentleman would do," he grinned.

There was no getting around it. Brendan would be Brendan, a booming, jovial Scotsman with flaming red hair and a personality to match. Dulcie sighed. "Yes, that'd be fine," she replied somewhat meekly, much to her own disgust.

Thankfully, he left her alone for a few moments as he went to the counter for more coffee. She finished her clean-up work, sat back in her chair, and once again attempted to relax.

Brendan returned. "Our waiter has said he will bring cappuccino over immediately, fine man that he is," Brendan said. Sitting again he looked deep into Dulcie's eyes. "How is it possible that you're bonnie eyes are even more beautiful?"

Dulcie put up her hand to stop him. "Okay, Brendan, as I said before, it is good to see you. But cut the crap. I know you, remember? You want to talk with me for a reason; this isn't just for old-time's sake. What brings you here?"

Brendan MacArthur pretended to look hurt by her accusation but knew he was no match for her when she was serious. He chuckled. "Perceptive, as always.

Of course, I did give myself away in my email. I do have a little project I've been working on." The waiter appeared with the coffee. "Ah, excellent! Good man!" Brendan's brogue was even thicker when he chose to be more 'authentic.' He knew how to use it to his advantage. "Nothin' like a fine brew!" he added, rolling out the R. "Except, a' course, a wee dram!" He winked at the waiter. He laughed, as Brendan had intended, and went back to the counter.

Dulcie sipped patiently. She had seen this many times. Brendan needed to wind himself down before he could get to the point.

"Ahhhh," he exhaled loudly after a long slurping sip and put down his cup. "So, my darling Dulcie. To be succinct, which I know you appreciate, I have a gift for you. Nay, a gift wrapped in a wee proposition!" He waited for the effect.

Dulcie continued to drink her coffee serenely.

"Ah, I see you are not falling for my proposals once again," he grinned. "Good girl. All right then. Here it is. But first, let me tell you a story."

"*Oh my God, Brendan!* Will you just get *on* with it?" Although she tried, Dulcie had never been an overly patient person.

Brendan knew he had her now. He put down his cup and leaned forward. "The year, my lass, is 1869. In the autumn of that year, there was a gale, a terrible gale! The winds swept up over the blue sea and the waves crashed, fierce with anger!"

Dulcie rolled her eyes. "Water doesn't get angry Brendan. Do you have a point?"

He ignored her. "They called it the Saxby Gale! Such a wind did howl that terrible night!"

Dulcie was shaking her head now. She looked at her watch purposefully.

"But, I see I have an unappreciative audience."

"You'll have no audience in a minute, Brendan. Get on with it," Dulcie said.

"Fine. The long and the short of it. A ship went down off one of your islands out in the bay during the Saxby Gale. Yours truly located it and…" he paused for effect. Dulcie sipped her coffee, unaffected. "… *and*," he repeated with emphasis, "along with the standard bits of cargo, we found a case of wine. Still intact. The wine, I mean."

Dulcie's cup hovered in mid-air. She looked intently at Brendan. "What kind?" she asked.

"Now I have your attention!" he replied, his eyebrows lifting. "It appears to be a Château Lafite Rothschild."

Dulcie set her cup down in the saucer carefully and deliberately. "Brendan," she said, "You know as well as I do that the chances of it being any good are slim. The corks will surely be damaged or crumbling. It'll be vinegar, or worse yet, seawater will have seeped in."

"Not necessarily! You see, Dulcie, I took the bold step of opening a bottle. What you have is, quite simply, something that nears perfection in my humble opinion!"

"Brendan, you've never been humble a day in your life," Dulcie laughed. "But I'll admit, it really does sound exciting! Why are you telling me this, however?"

"Because I'd like to donate a bottle to the museum," He replied simply. He sat back and waited for his words to sink in.

Dulcie paused. She toyed with her now empty cup. The implications began to dawn on her. A bottle of Château Lafite Rothschild. A bottle of century and a half old Château Lafite Rothschild. A bottle of century and a half old *drinkable* Château Lafite Rothschild. Her mind was churning with ideas. Then one thought popped into her head and she looked intently across the table at her former boyfriend. "Why?" she asked pointedly.

Brendan chuckled to himself. He knew Dulcie would get to that question sooner rather than later. He was prepared. "My lass, I would give you the usual guff about supporting a worthy cause and such, but you know me far too well, so I'll skip that part. What I am hoping for is a certain level of quiet publicity. I have more bottles, most of which have corks as intact as this first one. I plan to auction them. Do you know what the last lot similar to this sold for? Over $200,000. Per bottle."

Dulcie was silent. Something wasn't quite right, but she couldn't determine what, exactly, was bothering her. She needed more information. "Brendan, if I recall correctly, the spoils of a wreck belong to the state that has jurisdiction. If this is off the coast of an island out in the bay, it's in US waters. Specifically Maine waters. Doesn't that mean that the State of Maine actually owns this wine?"

He waved his hand in front of him as if to bat away an annoying fly. "It all depends on circumstances, lass. And who you know," he wiggled his eyebrows. "However, now that you mention it, I would like to keep this relatively quiet."

Dulcie understood. He wanted the knowledge to circulate among a certain level of society, but didn't want it to be overtly public. That level of society would be exactly the one that she dealt with regularly. The one with money to spare. Typically lots of it. They had a way of avoiding the details of their wealth when it came to the authorities just as Brendan was now doing.

"All right. Here's my thought," she replied. "We'll hold an 'intimate gathering' of a few museum patrons that I happen to know are wine enthusiasts. The evening will ostensibly be to have a private viewing of the new exhibit, but I'll circulate the rumor to a chosen few that there will be a very special bottle of wine that we would like them all to try."

Brendan nodded happily. "Perfect, my love. You are heaven incarnate!" His brogue had become thick again as he spoke.

"Not so fast, though," Dulcie continued. "I might want to invite a special guest."

Brendan pointed to himself and grinned.

"Uh, I mean other than you," Dulcie said. "I have a friend who runs the best wine bar in Portland. She said she just hired a guy who was invited to take the Master Sommelier exam. I want to invite him to come and give his expert opinion."

Brendan began to interrupt, looking concerned.

Dulcie stopped him. "Look, if the wine is as good as you say it is, he'll help your cause. If it isn't, you'll be spared perhaps one or two lawsuits."

Brendan was annoyed but nodded. He looked out the window, across the street. This wasn't going exactly as he had planned. He had forgotten what an adversary Dulcie could be.

Dulcie knew that she hadn't completely regained control of the situation, but had at least asserted a small amount of power. That's what was required with Brendan MacArthur. Now there was an element of surprise over which he had no control. '*Good*,' Dulcie thought. '*That gives me some leverage, at least.*'

The concerned look that had flitted into Brendan's starkly blue eyes was gone in an instant. "Of course, my dear Dulcie. You couldn't be more correct. I look forward to it!"

"I'm sure," Dulcie replied smoothly. She slid her empty cup away from her and reached for her coat on the back of the chair. "I'll be in touch with the details. I assume you'll be in town for a week or two?"

"Why, yes! Such lovely weather you're enjoying here. How could I leave now?" Brendan replied.

Dulcie smiled with what she realized was sincerity for the first time since he had arrived at the table. "Yes, not unlike Scotland, Maine has its own special charms in January."

Brendan snorted in reply. "You've yet to experience those charms while wearing a dry suit in the Atlantic during the winter. I believe I have that one on you, lassie," he said.

"That you do," Dulcie replied. "That you do!"

⋘

Jeremy Plunkett wiped off the bar in front of him as the couple he was about to serve commented loudly on the wines they saw displayed. "Oh that's just the *worst* year for that pinot!" the man announced. The young woman giggled and nodded. Jeremy could tell that she had no idea whether he was correct or not.

"Do you have something in mind or would you like a recommendation?" he asked the couple.

"Oh, a recommendation, of course!" the man said with a hint of sarcasm.

Jeremy had seen it before so many times. Someone who had a little knowledge but thought it applied to everything. He turned and picked up the bottle that the man had just maligned. "You are correct that 2011 was indeed a bad year, notably in California's Russian River Valley. However, this cabernet is from Napa where they thankfully enjoyed a bit of drier, warmer weather late in the season after the rains. I think you'll find it quite nice. Would you like to try some?" He smiled winningly. The man looked away. The young woman nodded eagerly.

Jeremy poured while thinking, '*Don't mess with me, dude. I've pulled all-nighters to learn this stuff. I'll be way ahead of you every time.'* He wasn't smug about his knowledge, it was simply a point of fact. He knew more. Period.

He needed to know all of it. Every last detail. The tiny room, probably intended as a closet, that he had converted into his study was covered with maps, charts, lists, notes, and anything else that would help him remember everything possible about wine. What had begun as a passion had long since evolved into an obsession. He tried to hide it from most people. He didn't want to appear strange. But like the kid who had memorized every baseball card of every player on every team for an entire decade, his knowledge just kept popping out of his mouth.

Jeremy turned away from the couple before he could say anything else and walked to the opposite end of the bar. A man had just come in and slid up onto a stool. Jeremy was about to ask him what he wanted when the man blurted out, "I don't know what I want. Bring me something white. Something fruity but not sweet." Jeremy thought for a moment. He pulled a bottle out from the refrigerator behind the bar and showed the man the label. The man shrugged in response and nodded. Jeremy poured.

The man inhaled over the glass, took a long, slow swig, swirled the liquid around in his mouth and swallowed. "Thank you," was all he said, then turned sideways to the bar, holding has glass and staring out the window. Jeremy had been effectively dismissed.

That was fine with him. He wiped the moisture from the cold bottle off his hands onto his crisp white apron, then retreated to the corner of the bar where he covertly pulled out a list of German appellations that he was trying to memorize. For some reason, the German language always tripped him up.

"Studying on the job?" the voice mad Jeremy jump. It was his boss, the owner of the wine bar, Veronica. She took the paper out of his hand and turned it around to look at it. "Good luck!" she smirked, handing it back to him.

Jeremy shook his head. "Yeah, I know. They all sound the same to me, dammit. I have no problem with Italian and French, but for some reason this gets me every time." He rattled the paper with annoyance.

"You need some kind of trick. A naming device or something to help you. Or a song, maybe."

"Do you know any songs about German wines?" Jeremy asked in disbelief.

"No, but I know some about the beer," Veronica replied, straightening the bottles on the shelf behind him. She stopped and turned to face him. "Hey, in other news, I have a favor to ask of you."

"Yeah?" Jeremy replied hesitantly. The last favor was working a double shift on a Saturday. He'd been exhausted for three days after and had lost valuable study time.

"Oh c'mon! You'll like this one!"

"Why do I not believe you?" Jeremy asked without looking up from his study sheet.

"It involves wine tasting, and it won't be here," she said in a taunting voice.

Jeremy's head jerked up. He stared intently.

Veronica laughed. "How would you like to be the guest sommelier at a posh little party where you get to try a 150 year old Château Lafite Rothschild?"

The study sheet slipped out of his fingers and fluttered to the floor. He ignored it. "What?" he nearly shouted.

"Oh, you heard me," Veronica leaned over and picked up the paper. She was a solid woman, and grunted softly as she straightened again. Handing the sheet back to him she said, "Here's the scoop. My friend is the director of the Maine Museum of Art. She's putting together a fundraiser for a new exhibit. Something about the ice age although I don't know how that plays into art," she started to trail off.

"Keep going, Veronica! Stay with me here!" Jeremy interjected.

She grinned. "Well it seems that someone is giving the museum a bottle of wine that they found in a shipwreck. The expected 'donation' to try it at the party is $5,000 a head, except for you my blessed friend. You have the great honor of tasting for free and giving your so-called expert opinion. And all because I recommended you!"

Jeremy was speechless. This was a fantastic opportunity. No one he knew had done anything like this, ever! The group he studied with for the upcoming exam would die of envy when they heard about this!

Veronica was still talking. "Of course it could be total crap in which case a lot of people would have shelled out some big bucks for nothing. But still…"

Jeremy couldn't focus. It was incredible. "I don't know what to say. Thank you, Veronica!"

"Okay, but I haven't given you the night off yet," she answered.

Jeremy's face fell. He looked like a forlorn puppy.

"I'm joking! Of course you can go! It'll be a good night out for you. And your weather-girl wife can look at the ice age art."

Jeremy hadn't even thought about Samantha. He knew he'd been neglecting her, but he had to stay focused. "Yeah. Actually it would be good to get out with her," he agreed.

"Excellent. Then it's settled. Here's my friend's card. Get in touch with her and get the details."

Jeremy took the card, reached into his back pocket, pulled out his wallet, and carefully placed the card inside. Then he stuffed the wallet as far back down in his pocket as it would go.

From where he was seated at the bar, Patrick Spratt had heard the entire conversation. His mind was spinning. This was it, the perfect opportunity.

His family had long been connected with the museum. His grandmother had funded an entire wing. The Spratt name was built on very old money, dating back to fortunes made in shipping during the American Revolution. That was about as far back as you could go in the US.

Patrick didn't often play that card, but when required he could easily use it to his advantage. He finished his wine, an excellent New Zealand Sauvignon blanc, put a fifty dollar bill on the bar, and quietly slipped out.

Great things are done by a series
of small things brought together.

~ Vincent van Gogh

CHAPTER FOUR

Patrick listened to the buzzing sound of the phone on the other end of the line ringing three, four, five times and was about to give up when a cranky voice answered.

"Hullo?" It was low and raspy, as though the speaker had enjoyed one too many glasses of scotch the night before.

"Uncle Geoffrey! Did I wake you?" Patrick asked.

"What the hell time is it! Middle of the night still!"

"Uncle Geoffrey, it's about ten o'clock in the morning," Patrick replied smoothly. He heard a grunt from the other end of the line.

Geoffrey Spratt was the brother of Patrick's father. Both of his parents had died when Patrick was very young, and Geoffrey had raised him, if one could call it that. What he had done was set strict rules for behavior while Patrick was in his house, then shipped the boy off to boarding school so that he was underfoot as little as possible. Geoffrey was a confirmed bachelor. He had never really liked children. Or most anyone, for that matter.

From an early age, however, Patrick had developed a natural charm which cast itself as innocence. He was well aware of this. He had learned to win his uncle over, quite easily in fact. Beneath Geoffrey Spratt's gruff exterior, he adored Patrick. Geoffrey had come to think of his nephew nearly as a son.

"Uncle, I have a question. Do you still know anyone over at the art museum?" Patrick already knew the answer. Of course Uncle Geoffrey did. He knew the entire board of directors. A check from Geoffrey Spratt would render them biddable at any given moment.

"Of course I do. What do you need?" Geoffrey had no trouble getting to the heart of the matter as quickly as possible.

Patrick took a deep breath. "I've just heard that they have a new exhibit opening that's right down my alley. Paintings of the Little Ice Age," he answered, diverting the point slightly.

"What the hell is that?" the older man barked.

"It was a period of time between the 14th and the 19th centuries when it was colder in Europe, so winters lasted longer and bodies of water froze so solidly that people could travel across them." Patrick uttered the words in a steady stream knowing that his uncle wouldn't care.

"What's that got to do with me?" Geoffrey croaked.

Patrick considered for a moment. Should he play all of his cards now, or just the few needed to gain an invitation to the museum event? "I was hoping that you could help me get an invitation to the fundraiser that kicks off the exhibit. I'm very interested in it, as you can imagine."

Geoffrey was silent. He thought the world of his nephew, but he knew him, too. There had to be a catch. "Why not just wait until the thing opens officially?" he asked pointedly.

'*All right,*' Patrick thought. '*Might as well spill it now. He'll find out sooner or later.*' He took a deep breath. "To be honest, I know that Sam will be there, and I want to talk to her."

Now Geoffrey was fully awake. He paused. He had liked Samantha. True, she wasn't of the same level as the Spratt family, but she had the brains and the looks to make up for that. '*Good breeding stock,*' his family would have said. It was intended as a compliment.

Geoffrey had thought his nephew behaved like an idiot when he had broken off the relationship with Samantha. At the time, he had made his opinion quite clear. Now he scratched his head in an effort to think more quickly. "What do you want to talk to her about?" he asked.

"I'm not really sure," Patrick answered. "Look, I know I was stupid and made a big mistake. And it was a huge shock to see her on TV."

"To all of us!" Geoffrey agreed.

"But that's just made me think about her even more," Patrick admitted.

"So you're thinking of getting her back?" Geoffrey asked. This was the closest thing to a heart-to-heart discussion that he had ever had with his nephew.

"That's just it. I can't. She's been married for a couple of years at least."

"What?" Geoffrey acknowledged. "How'd that happen? I mean, seems awfully quick after the two of you were together for so long,"

"Yeah, I know," Patrick agreed. "She really is the one, though, isn't she Uncle Geoffrey."

Geoffrey Spratt didn't know what to say. Deep and meaningful conversations were not his forte. But he had taken a liking to the girl and did think that she was the kind of influence that Patrick needed. "Couples don't necessarily last," was all he could come up with. "She could become single again. Hell, maybe she's working on it right now!" His attempt at humor fell somewhat flat.

Patrick sighed. "I won't bet on it," he said simply. "But for now, can you get me an invitation to that party?" His tone was wistful.

Uncle Geoffrey cleared his throat. "Sure thing, kid. No worries. Count on your ol' Uncle."

"Thanks, Uncle Geoffrey. You've always been there for me. I really appreciate it." Patrick didn't want to lay it on too thick.

"You've worked hard. No one deserves it more than you," Geoffrey said. He grunted a salutation and hung up the phone.

Patrick carefully put his phone down. He went over to the window and looked out across the dirty snow and the ice-covered sidewalk. He would get her back. He would do anything to get her back.

❧

"When does your charming brother arrive?" Rachel asked while simultaneous typing on her computer.

Dulcie was always amazed that Rachel seemed to be able to do multiple things at the same time, yet she never appeared to be flustered about anything. *I need to give her a raise,'* Dulcie thought. *'If I lose her, I'm sunk.'*

Rachel paused and looked up at Dulcie, waiting for an answer. "Oh, sorry Rachel. Just thinking for a second. Dan? He flies back tomorrow morning. And I have to say, he's not entirely happy about it."

Rachel looked back at her laptop screen and began to type again. "Not happy about coming back to the frozen tundra that we now live in, or not happy about leaving the sophisticated Miami social scene?" she giggled.

"Both, I imagine!" Dulcie answered. "I'll be glad to see him again. He's coming to the party tomorrow night, of course, and I'm much more comfortable with him there."

"He sure knows how to work a room," Rachel agreed.

"Much better than I can," Dulcie said.

Rachel was sitting at the opposite side of Dulcie's desk. She closed her laptop and peered over it at her boss. "I don't know about that. You do really well. You always seem very relaxed and chatty."

"Years of practice." Dulcie said, not looking up from her own computer. "And numerous tips from my brother." Now she did look up. "I've never been comfortable with it, though. You know that. I wish I had Dan's ease."

"But if you did, you might not have some of the other qualities that make you so good at the rest of your job," Rachel replied. She stood and slid her computer under her arm. "Anything more you need from me for now?"

Dulcie shook her head. "Thanks for finishing those emails. I think now we're just on to the details for tomorrow."

Rachel nodded, smiled, and went out the door, her unruly red curls springing out of her polka-dot headband and bouncing on her shoulders.

Dulcie reached up and smoothed her own straight dark hair into the clip that held it back. She'd been wearing it like this often as of late. *'I should wear it down tomorrow night, just for a change,'* she thought. It reminded her that she had not planned what she would wear yet. Experience had taught her that she would inevitably run out of time and have little left to get herself ready. She thought about the black dress that she had fallen back on for several previous events. Surely everyone had seen it by now. Did it really matter, though?

Then she remembered who would be attending. Nick of course. And Brendan. "That's just great," she said aloud sarcastically. But, she was a grown woman after all, right? She could certainly handle the situation.

A new dress wouldn't hurt, though, and might give her a little confidence boost. *'Seriously? Are you that shallow?'* she argued with herself. *'I don't care. If I want a new damn dress, I'm going to buy a new damn dress!'*

She closed her computer firmly and stood before she could change her mind. Sliding into her coat she picked up her purse and nearly ran through the door of her office. She breezed by Rachel. "Hold my calls, please. I'm going dress shopping."

"OOOOhhhhh!" Rachel squealed from behind her. "I would so love to see this!" Dulcie was not known for taking risks with her wardrobe.

"Shut up," Dulcie tossed back over her shoulder. "I might just surprise you!" She pulled on her gloves, slipped her hood over her head and pushed through the heavy double doors of the museum.

A biting wind slammed into her when she stepped outside. She gripped her hood to hold it in place. Her knee-high leather boots were obviously made for fashion and not for the cold. She stomped down the street in an effort to keep her feet warm as she made her way toward a nearby dress shop.

As soon as she entered, a waft of potpourri hit her nostrils, and she sneezed. *'Good start,'* she thought. Removing her gloves, she pulled out a tissue from her pocket, covertly wiped her nose, then shoved gloves and tissue back into her coat. She unbuttoned the heavy wool and began to tackle the rack of dresses in front of her.

The hangers screeched on the rod as Dulcie flicked through the clothes. One dress caught her eye and she pulled it out. It was a dark garnet red, an unusual color for her to choose, with a longer flowing skirt, bracelet length sleeves, and a deep V-neckline. She walked over to the mirror and held it up in front of her.

"That would look really nice on you," a quiet voice said from behind her.

Dulcie turned, expecting to see one of the store clerks, but instead found herself gazing at a familiar, yet unfamiliar, face. "Thanks. It's a little outside of my comfort zone," she said, "but maybe it's time to shake things up a little?" she added skeptically.

The woman laughed softly. "I know all about that!" she said.

Dulcie continued to stare at her. "I'm sorry," she finally said. "I know you from somewhere but I can't place you. I'm the art museum director, so I meet a lot of people and I'm terrible with names, unfortunately."

The woman smiled. "No, we haven't met. You might have seen me giving the weather forecast, though."

The weather girl - that was it! '*No*,' Dulcie admonished herself. '*Weather Forecaster!*'

The woman was still talking. "We were going to meet soon, though. I mean, I think we would have. My husband and I are coming to the event tomorrow night at the museum. I'm Samantha Sanders." She held out her hand and shook Dulcie's quickly.

Dulcie was surprised. She was sure that she had not seen Samantha's name on the guest list. She made it a point to memorize them as much as possible so she would be prepared with any bits of small talk that might be appropriate. "That's wonderful! Does your husband have the same last name? I don't remember seeing it…"

Samantha shook her head vigorously. "No, his name is Jeremy Plunkett."

Now it made sense. Neither of them had been on the guest list originally. "Our official sommelier!" Dulcie exclaimed. "My friend Veronica recommended him. I didn't realize that he was married to a celebrity!"

A pink blush crept up over Samantha's cheeks. She turned to hang up one of the dresses she was holding, hoping that Dulcie wouldn't notice. "Not really a celebrity. I just forecast the weather."

Forecast. So had Dulcie been right saying she was a *weather forecaster*? Maybe now wasn't the best time to ask. "Well, I'm very glad you can come. Are you looking for a new dress to wear tomorrow, too?"

Samantha nodded. She held up a simple navy blue silk sheath. It was exactly what Dulcie would have chosen for herself, except that Samantha's hourglass shape would certainly fill it out much more seductively. She glanced at the other woman then back at the dress. A thought popped into her head. *'She has absolutely no idea how alluring she is.'*

"You would look great in that," Dulcie said aloud.

"Thanks. I know it's pretty plain, but I don't like to draw attention to myself. I already get too much attention as it is." The words were not said in false modesty.

"I think it would be perfect. Besides, you husband should be getting the bulk of the attention, at least for part of the evening."

Samantha brightened for a moment. "That's true. Plus, I want to sneak away and just look at the paintings. I'm more interested in the exhibit than any of that wine business. I've been studying historical climate change."

"Now that's interesting! I'll take you on a personal tour when you arrive," Dulcie replied. She turned back to the mirror. "Do you think it's too much? I'm not usually a red person."

Samantha laughed. "I think you're about to become one," she said.

ॐ

In his hotel room, Brendan MacArthur was carefully pressing his suit. He thought about Dulcie. Had he given her enough time to get the word out? He knew how efficient she was, so the answer was probably a *yes*.

Brendan had planned everything down to the last detail. The quick conversation with Dulcie. The limited time before the event. All this would add up to many breathless conversations over a very short period of time, and that would stir up interest, along with plenty of gossip, about the Château Lafite Rothschild.

He thought about his recent dive in the icy Maine waters. It had been a bit of a risk to go down at this time of year, but he had to retrieve the rest of the bottles quickly if he was going to sell them. He hadn't told his diving buddies much about the wine, other than to say that he thought it might be worth something. They knew what that could mean.

The only part of the venture that he didn't like was sharing the profits. He never enjoyed that. Brendan had come from money. He delighted in money. He spent it at a nearly reckless pace. Coming by more was increasingly a problem.

He looked across the room at the one bottle he had with him. The rest were safely hidden away. It reminded him of the other problem that he had, even greater than sharing the spoils. Had he taken care of that sufficiently?

An acrid smell brought him back to his senses and he quickly lifted the iron off the pant leg it had been resting on. A faint, triangular imprint remained pressed into the expensive Italian wool fabric. "Dammit," Brendan muttered. He turned around, picked up the phone and called the hotel concierge. He would know what to do about it. They knew everything. Brendan shook his head slightly thinking, '*Should have left it with him in the first place instead of ironing myself.*' He had always hated ironing but, when forced to economize, sending out clothes simply to be freshened and pressed was an extravagance. He despised economizing.

Creativity is allowing yourself to make mistakes.
Art is knowing which ones to keep.
~ Scott Adams

CHAPTER FIVE

"Dulcie, what do we have in store tonight?" The voice boomed into Dulcie's office followed by a very tanned Dan Chambers. She stood up from her desk, gave him a quick hug, and promptly sat down again.

"Dan you look fabulous. And relaxed, although I've never seen you actually tense so that's nothing new. Had fun, I assume?" She was reading through a list of names as she spoke.

"Absolutely. Excellent time. Could not have enjoyed it more. I swam in shark infested waters every day."

"Mmmmm?" Dulcie replied, then looked up sharply. "What?!"

"Just kidding. Thought that might get your attention. I'll tell you all about it later. What can I do for you right now, though?"

Dulcie exhaled loudly. She was tense, a typically feeling for her on the day of an event. "Please tell me that you're coming tonight, and that you can get here early?" She asked.

"Always do," Dan said.

"Good. Thanks. Sorry I'm distracted. I'm dealing with a last minute addition to the program that's all good, of course. Well, mostly good, but frankly it has nothing to do with the exhibit," she blurted out quickly.

Dan raised his eyebrows but was silent. He knew that when Dulcie spoke at a rapid pace, she was trying not to say something.

Dulcie hesitated. "Okay, fine. Brendan MacArthur is here."

A grin swept across Dan's face. "Brendan! Wow! How long has it been?" He and Brendan were two of a kind, revelers from birth. When Dan had visited Dulcie in England, Brendan had spent more time with him than with Dulcie. "So what's the problem with that?" he asked, finally noticing that Dulcie was not smiling.

Dulcie sat back in her chair. "He just... he just seems to take over. It was fun at first with him. Plus, we were in school, so it didn't really matter. But then it got old because whenever he was around, it was Brendan's world and anyone else was simply along for the ride," she replied.

"Now you're the one who's in charge, though. This is your museum," he gestured around the room.

"I know, and you're right, but here's the thing. He *will* actually be the center of attention tonight. He's donating a bottle of wine that he found in a shipwreck off Cliff Island, and it's supposedly drinkable. A one hundred and fifty year old Château Lafite Rothschild."

Dan let out a long, low whistle.

"I know!" Dulcie continued. "So I've turned the event tonight into a fundraiser as well as a preview of the new exhibit. Those who can afford it will be able to taste the wine."

"Wait a second, why would he donate something like that? It's obviously valuable," Dan wondered. "I think he's a good guy, but I'm not sure he's that selfless."

"He isn't. He has more that he plans to sell to the highest bidder."

The realization dawned on Dan. "So this is a marketing ploy for him!" he exclaimed. "Have to say, that's pretty clever."

"Brendan excels at clever," Dulcie quipped.

"You can say that again," said Dan. "But getting back to the tasting, can I ask exactly what 'afford it' means?"

"A five thousand dollar donation to the museum," Dulcie said without hesitation. She had grown used to talking about large sums of money. In comparison, this one wasn't even very big.

"Holy cow! I'm out then!" Dan laughed but then looked at Dulcie more seriously. "You know it could be total crap. Won't they be annoyed if it is?"

"Maybe," Dulcie said. "But that's the risk they take. What they're really paying for is the chance to go into the board room with other people who have shelled out five grand each and pretend they all know something about wine."

"Some of them might," Dan countered. He was always the diplomat.

"Yes, you're right. Some of them. And, I'm allowing the ones who don't the opportunity to save face. I'm bringing in a professional sommelier to give his expert opinion first."

"Do you know if it's any good at all? Has anyone tried it?" Dan asked.

"Brendan has. He says it's good. He's no somm, but he does know a lot about wine. And it pains me to admit that his palette is better than mine," Dulcie grimaced.

"You sound like such a snob now, Dulcie!" Dan stood up and headed for the door. "No worries, though. I'll keep Brendan well occupied and out of your hair." He stopped in the doorway and turned back around. "But I do it for a price," he added.

"Really?" Dulcie said suspiciously. "What's that?"

"I get to taste the wine, too. I figure reigning in that rowdy Scotsman is worth at least the equivalent of five grand."

"It's actually worth more, but I'll never admit to that," Dulcie replied. "Thanks, Dan" she added.

"Anytime," he said, sauntering away. Dulcie heard Rachel's giggle from the gallery outside and just shook her head. Dan would never stop being the flirt.

Dulcie locked her office door, drew the shade and walked over to the small closet in the corner. She opened it and carefully pulled out the new red dress. She took a deep breath, holding it up in front of her and looking down at it. "I suppose I have no other options," she murmured. She had deliberately brought only this one dress so that she wouldn't be able to change her mind at the last moment.

She slipped off her clothes and quickly put it in, barely being able to zip it up in the back on her own. She pulled on stockings, hiking them up underneath the skirt. After slipping on her pumps, she finally allowed herself to look in the full-length mirror inside the closet door. Now she saw that she had managed to get the hem of her skirt stuck in the waistband of her hose, exposing her underwear. "Good job!" she told herself sarcastically.

She pulled the skirt out and fluffed it around her, looking in the mirror again. "Not bad," she finally admitted aloud. It certainly was very red. *'If I'm going to withstand Brendan MacArthur though, I'll need all the red I can get,'* she thought. She brushed her hair and pulled the top and sides back into a barrette leaving the rest down. A little eyeliner and mascara finished the job. *'There,'* she thought. *'Quite presentable.'*

The skirt wafted around her legs as she walked toward the window and opened the shade again. Continuing to the door, she unlocked and opened it just as Rachel was about to knock.

With her hand still held up she stepped back. Her eyes opened widely. "Wow!" she said. "You clean up good!"

Dulcie snorted. "Trying to push myself a little here," she admitted.

"And I'm sure having an ex-boyfriend and a current boyfriend at the same event has nothing to do with it?" Rachel asked sweetly.

"Do not push your luck," Dulcie said with narrowed eyes, but then laughed. "Seriously, does it work?" she asked looking down at herself.

Rachel nodded. "Totally works. You're not wearing earrings, though?"

"Arghh," Duclie exclaimed. She went back to her desk and dug through her purse until she found the white gold studs she'd plucked from her jewelry box at the last second that morning. "Okay, done!" she said checking herself one last time in the mirror before closing the closet door.

"Perfect," Rachel added. "The belle of the ball. Now back to work." She handed Dulcie a clipboard. "Revised guest list. We got a couple of last-minute phone calls. Plus two more checks for the wine tasting. Are we gonna have enough of that stuff?" she asked.

"I didn't think that would actually be a problem, but now…," she glanced at the number of names on the list and nodded. "I think we will. We managed to locate what are probably the smallest glasses in the city of Portland. We should be okay, just barely. I'll go without, and I'll make Dan do the same if need be."

"Dan donated *five thousand dollars*?" Rachel exclaimed.

"No. Long story. You don't want to know," Dulcie muttered, looking over the list more closely. "Huh! Geoffrey Spratt? Haven't seen him in a while. And this is his nephew, I think? Patrick?"

"Right," Rachel replied looking at where Dulcie was pointing. "Don't think we've ever seen him here before. Not that I know of anyway. As for Uncle Geoffrey, I didn't know he ventured forth in the winter. I've never seen him at anything but a summer event. Figured he went somewhere like the sunny Caribbean, or at least Florida, at the first hint of frost."

"Me too," Dulcie replied thoughtfully. She handed the list back to Rachel. "All right. To your battle stations!"

Rachel giggled as Dulcie headed toward the main gallery. She drifted forward in a red cloud, looking like she had just stepped out of an Italian Renaissance painting.

"You look stunning!" A voice whispered from behind Dulcie as she felt a hand touch her back. She whirled around and smiled at Nick.

"And you're looking quite dapper yourself!" she agreed.

"I hope you don't mind that I brought…," he didn't have time to finish the sentence before Johnson came clomping up behind him.

"Dulcie! Great to see you! You're looking fantastic! Really!" He cleared his throat. The pause was obvious.

Dulcie suddenly remembered. The weight loss clinic. "Never mind me Adam, you are looking quite svelte!" It was a blatant lie, but Johnson beamed anyway. He visibly sucked in his stomach.

"Been working hard on it, and I must say, I'm feeling very fit! The wife says she doesn't even recognize me!" He leaned toward Dulcie. "I even had to buy new pants!" He whispered loudly.

Dulcie thought she heard Nick groan. "Adam, you should be quite proud of yourself. You've done very well. Losing weight isn't easy."

Johnson nodded emphatically. He was eyeing the hors d'oeuvres already. "Is that shrimp I see? Good source of protein and low in fat. Be right back!" He moved speedily toward the table.

Dulcie turned to Nick. "How long do you give him before he's wearing the old pants again?" she asked.

"Six months, max," he grinned. "But 'A' for effort!" He scanned the room. His face darkened. "Which one is our guest of honor?" he asked.

"I'd hardly call him that," Dulcie answered. "He's over there, talking to Dan." She pointed as inconspicuously as she could.

As though they both had heard her, they looked over. "Dammit," breathed Dulcie. "Here they come."

Nick sized up Brendan MacArthur as he confidently strode across the room. *'Cocky'* was the first word that popped into his head. Nick had learned to trust first impressions.

As the two men reached them, Brendan leaned in and gave Dulcie a firm kiss on the cheek. "Aye, there's me lassie!" he exclaimed. "And looking as bonnie and bright as the sunset over Skye!"

In spite of herself, Dulcie blushed. Nick noticed. Now he was annoyed.

Dan stepped in. "Nick! Good to see you again! He stuck his arm in front of Brendan, effectively separating him from Dulcie, and shook Nick's hand. "Been at the boat show down in Florida. Saw a couple of yachts I wouldn't mind having!" He was still pumping Nick's fist. As he finally let go he gestured toward Brendan who had to step back so that he wouldn't be hit by Dan's flying arm. "Oh, sorry about my manners! Dulcie's always telling me to be more polite. This is a friend from across the pond. Brendan Macarthur. Brendan, this is Nicholas Black, Dulcie's boyfriend."

Dulcie realized that she'd been holding her breath and exhaled as quietly as possible. She looked at Dan and quickly mouthed, *'thank you'* as the two others shook hands. She was grateful that Dan had worked in the word *'boyfriend'* getting some of the awkwardness out of the way.

"You have a good one here, and that's no lie," Brendan announced. "I was sad to have lost her," he added.

Nick didn't like Brendan's comments. He didn't like Brendan. Something about him seemed disingenuous, in spite of the fact that he looked sincere. Nick filed it away for future reference.

"I hear you're a diver," he said, blatantly changing the subject.

"Aye! Love being on the sea and in the sea! And I've been diving in every one of our seven seas. It's a hobby that's gone mad," he replied, raking his hand through his roguish red hair. He looked over at Dulcie and winked.

She jumped in. "Brendan has made it more than a hobby, though. He's turned wreck diving into a career," she said.

'*Yeah, because he sells all the spoils that he can,*' thought Nick. "That's the best way to go about it," he replied instead. "Turn a hobby into a career."

"Exactly what I did," Dan added. "Hasn't made me rich, but then I can rarely complain, either. Hey," he looked across the room and waved at someone. "Is that Johnson? Or his thinner brother?" Johnson approached grinning.

"Must be his buff brother!" Johnson replied holding an enormous plate of shrimp.

Before Dulcie could introduce Adam Johnson to Brendan she saw Dan look across the room again. His jaw dropped. "Wow! Is that who I think it is?"

Dulcie turned around. She noticed that half the room had done the same. Mostly the male half. Taking off her coat and accepting a glass of champagne was Samantha Sanders. Her blonde hair cascaded down her back in a mass of curls. The plain sheath that Dulcie had seen her with at the dress shop fitted her curves like a glove. Her skin glowed and she smiled softly, almost shyly, as the man beside her spoke to the waiter carrying the tray of champagne. *'She has absolutely no idea of her effect,'* Dulcie thought. She glanced at Nick. He was staring at the woman too, but not in the same way as Dan or Brendan.

'Victim' was the word that entered Nick's head now. It was an odd word to apply to a woman how obviously had so much presence that she could gain the attention of an entire room without even speaking. That kind of presence was usually synonymous with power. Not in this case, Nick believed.

Suddenly remembering, Dan snapped his fingers loudly. The sound seemed to break the spell for everyone around him. "I know who that is! It's the Weather Girl!" he exclaimed.

"Weather Forecaster," Nick and Dulcie both corrected at once. They glanced at each other, trying not to smile.

Dulcie cleared her throat. "That's our sommelier for tonight as well. Excuse me gentlemen, I need to speak with them." She had effectively dismissed them, even Nick. This was her job, after all.

"Samantha! Good to see you again! And you must be Jeremy," they heard her say. She guided the two across the room, talking the entire time. Nick noticed that she moved them as far away as possible. He knew that it was not because she feared Dan's reaction. Dan may have been known for his appreciation of women, but he never overstepped the bounds of decorum. Dulcie must have had another reason for steering clear.

Then Nick looked over at Brendan. He was still staring. His eyes gleamed like a predator on the hunt, waiting to pounce, his prey in sight.

This was certainly going to be an interesting night, Nick thought. He tried to catch Johnson's eye to see if he had noticed the same thing. Unfortunately, he was too engrossed in his shrimp.

Dulcie moved Jeremy and Samantha toward the opposite end of the room. She had just explained the logistics of the evening. Jeremy kept nodding eagerly as she spoke. He looked like a puppy in anticipation of a new toy or a treat.

Samantha appeared distracted. *'I should take her into the gallery,'* Dulcie thought. *'She wanted to see the exhibit, and she looks so uncomfortable here.'*

Dulcie was about to suggest this when Nick approached. "So you're the expert sommelier!" he offered, somehow recognizing Dulcie's unease. Nick introduced himself. "I'd love to get your opinion on some vintages. Do you have a few minutes?"

Did he have a few minutes. The thought nearly made Samantha sneer, and she was not the sneering type. Jeremy had no time for anything but wine. She put her half-finished glass of champagne on a nearby table as if to protest.

"Would you like a quick tour of the exhibit?" Dulcie asked quietly. She sensed Samantha's annoyance. No, annoyance wasn't the correct term,

Dulcie realized. It was more of an attitude of unhappy resignation.

Samantha had been staring at the floor. She looked up at Dulcie quickly. "Oh, thank you! I'd love to!"

They walked quietly into the first gallery. Only a few people had wandered in to see the artworks, drifting quietly from painting to painting. Dulcie let Samantha drift for a few moments as well. It was the best way to take in an exhibit. Whatever Dulcie could tell her about each individual work wasn't nearly as important as what each painting made Samantha think and feel. It was that very affect that Dulcie loved about art. It could resonate on so many different levels.

Samantha paused in front of one of the paintings. It was a Henry Raeburn work from the 1790s. "*The Skating Minister*," Dulcie said quietly. "That's the unofficial title. He's skating on a loch in Scotland," she added.

Samantha eyed it more closely. "He doesn't look very happy. Then again, he doesn't look unhappy, either." She laughed nervously.

"I think he just looks determined," Dulcie said. "He isn't wearing a very thick coat so I can't imagine he's very warm. Maybe he's trying to get across that lake as quickly as possible?"

Samantha nodded. "I know the feeling. Kind of." She stepped back and looked around the room. "This is all so lovely. Serene. Really different from what I face each day."

"The weather isn't serene?" Dulcie said with mock surprise.

"Sometimes it is, but TV certainly isn't," Samantha explained. She quickly turned and faced Dulcie. "It was never what I wanted," she blurted out. "I was going to go into research. I was going to observe and study and write papers and make elaborate computer models. I don't know how this all happened." She shook her head sadly.

"Life," Dulcie said. "It's what happens when we're least ready for it." She hesitated for a moment. "Do you think that you still want those things?"

Samantha nodded emphatically. "I really do, but I'm stuck. Jeremy is trying to move his career forward with the sommelier credentials. Until that happens, I'm the breadwinner of the family," she nearly growled. "I agreed to it, but I didn't think it would take this long. I didn't think he would ignore everything else."

'*And everyone?*' thought Dulcie. She knew it had to be difficult, to put your own dreams on hold for someone else's. Then, to have your efforts unappreciated, which seemed to be the case here. That would make anyone bitter, at least temporarily.

She decided to change the subject. "What's the focus of your research, when you get back to it?" she asked.

Samantha brightened. "It's part of this," she gestured around her. "There were actually three cold periods in the Little Ice Age. They started in 1650, 1770, and 1850. I'm researching the last one. Or I hope to be, anyway."

"Interesting. So, cutting to the chase as I always do, what caused it?"

Samantha shook her head. "We don't really know but there are several strong theories. The one I'm working on involves the North Atlantic Oscillation. It's an air current that's considered either positive or negative. When it's negative, cold arctic air from Russia filters over Northern Europe toward the Mediterranean. When I get back to my research, I want to set up various computer models to test some ideas I have." Samantha spoke quickly but with the smooth authority of someone who knew, and enjoyed, her subject very well.

'She really is living the wrong life right now,' Dulcie thought. "It's great to meet someone who loves their work as much as I do," she observed aloud.

They continued around the room then approached the doorway again. The crowd had grown since they had been in the gallery. Both women hesitated for a moment, looking into the next room.

Samantha suddenly stiffened. Dulcie looked sideways at her. Samantha's face was gray and her mouth had fallen open slightly. Dulcie touched her arm. "Samantha? Are you all right?" She jumped at Dulcie's touch and swallowed hard. Looking at the floor, Samantha inhaled deeply, as though she couldn't get enough air to breathe. "Do you want to sit down?" Dulcie asked. Samantha nodded and they retreated to a bench back in the gallery.

"What's wrong?" Dulcie questioned. "You saw a ghost, I think!"

Samantha gulped again. "Sort of. It's a long story. I just, well, I saw someone that I didn't want to see again. Ever. I don't know why he'd be here."

"Who is it? I know everyone on the guest list. Maybe I can help?"

Samantha took another deep breath. "Patrick Spratt," she replied flatly.

Dulcie thought for a moment. "He and his uncle were last-minute additions," she said. "Geoffrey Spratt has been a very big donor to the museum over the years. The whole Spratt family has. Evidently he learned about the wine tasting because he made the requested donation for him and his nephew Patrick to attend. They'll be up in the boardroom with the others a bit later." She looked intently at Samantha. "Will that be a problem for you? I know Jeremy is taking part, but you don't need to be there if…"

"I *won't* let him intimidate me!" Samantha snapped.

'Whew! Bit of history there!' Dulcie thought. "I understand," she said aloud. "Do what you're most comfortable with. I need to go back out there," she added while standing. "Stay in here where it's more quiet for as long as you like, though."

"I'm sorry. I'll be fine," Samantha replied. "I just need to compose myself. I'll be out in a moment."

Dulcie nodded and left.

As she walked back into the main hall she checked her watch. Fifteen minutes until the tasting. Only a few of the guests would be participating. Dulcie wanted them to slip away as quietly as possible. She needed to circulate through the room, locate each one, and direct them upstairs to the boardroom.

She began with Brendan, spotting him nearby. "Ah, Dulcie!" Brendan said as she approached. To Dulcie's surprise, he slipped an arm around her waist and pulled her tightly against has side. "Just talking about you, love!" he announced. His speech was slurred slightly.

Dulcie tried to pull herself away without being too obvious. Nick was at her side instantly. "Trouble?" he whispered.

Dulcie found herself feeling annoyed. First Samantha was affected by the mere presence of Patrick Spratt. Dulcie had no idea what the history was, but clearly he had some menacing hold over Samantha. Then Brendan treated Dulcie in what only could be described as a patronizing manner. And now Nick was swooping in as though she couldn't handle things. "No, everything's fine," she barked. Nick stepped away slightly, taken aback.

Brendan had just lifted another drink from the tray of a passing waiter. Dulcie had seen him drinking on many occasions in the past. He was always jovial, loud, the life of the party, especially as he continued to drink. However, that was not the atmosphere that Dulcie wanted or expected here. She took his arm, smiled at his companions, and said, "Do you mind if I drag this gentleman away for a moment?" They nodded, without missing a beat in their conversation.

Dulcie took Brendan's drink and placed it on a table as they continued walking. She smiled but her voice was severe. "Brendan, no more. You have a very big event that's about to happen. Let's stay clear, shall we?"

He just grinned.

"Wait here," she said. She waived to Jeremy who joined them. "I'm going to take you upstairs, then find the participants. Can you two make sure everything is ready? I think Rachel is up there now." She marched them quickly upstairs, then came back down. Nick was waiting at the landing.

"Anything wrong?" he asked. "Can I help?"

Dulcie sighed. She'd been harsh, and it wasn't necessarily his fault. She was just annoyed with men in general at the moment. They seemed to be either intimidating or rescuing, as though their sole purpose was to play the King or the Knight in Shining Armor. "Yes, you can. Could you go up to the board room and keep an eye on things? Rachel is in charge until I get there. And bring Adam, too? For some reason, I feel as though we're spinning a bit out of control here." She quelled her feelings regarding the Knight in Shining Armor. After all, she didn't think Rachel could strong-arm a tipsy Brendan if that's what was required. For that matter, she wasn't even sure Nick could. Johnson's bulk, although slightly reduced, might be needed.

"Will do," he said over his shoulder, already locating Johnson who was finishing his second plate of shrimp.

Dulcie scanned the room. Geoffrey Spratt was nearby talking with his nephew and three others who had donated for the tasting. She glided in beside Geoffrey, politely interrupted, and directed them upstairs. *'Good,'* she sighed. *'Only a few more to go.'*

Next she found Samantha. "Are you feeling up to this, or do you want to pass?" Dulcie asked quietly. "I've just sent Patrick and his uncle upstairs."

Samantha blinked several times, but then straightened her shoulders. "No, I'm up to it. I should be supportive of my husband, right? I mean, that's what a good wife would do." Sarcasm had edged into her voice.

Dulcie chose to ignore it. She didn't think Samantha had intended for her to hear it. Actually, she didn't think Samantha realized it was there. "I'll be going in last after I've rounded up everyone. Want to slip in with me? It'll take me about five more minutes."

Samantha nodded. "I'll watch for you. Thanks."

In fewer than five minutes Dulcie had sent the last of the elite group upstairs to the boardroom. Samantha was already beside her. "Thank you, again. I'm in a difficult situation. You have no idea how much this helps!" Samantha admitted.

Dulcie was curious but had no time to ask for the whole story. Perhaps she didn't want to hear it anyway. Everyone had a story; there was something unsavory in everyone's past.

They entered the boardroom. The heavy oak tables had been rearranged to allow people to stand rather than sit as they would at a meeting. Only one table remained at the center of the room. Rachel was standing at the end of it with Jeremy on one side of her and Brendan on the other. Dulcie noted that Nick and Johnson had flanked them as well but were back several paces. She nearly giggled thinking that they almost looked like Secret Service agents keeping a watchful eye on everyone.

Samantha quickly found Jeremy and stood slightly behind him. She was relieved to see that Patrick was on the opposite side of the room.

Dulcie joined Rachel.

"Thank you, everyone, for coming tonight!" Dulcie said loudly, gaining the group's attention. The room fell silent. "And thank you for your more than generous donations. Winter is a difficult time in Maine, as you all know! Museum attendance is always low this time of year, so I'm very pleased to provide the motivation to bring everyone out on a cold night." Several people chuckled and one responded with a hearty "Hear Hear!"

Dulcie smiled and continued. "We are grateful to a new friend of the museum, Mr. Brendan MacArthur, for donating such a valuable gift and giving us the opportunity to share this experience," she turned to Brendan. "Could you tell us about how you found this wine?" she asked. She prayed that he wouldn't elaborate too much.

"Aye! I would be happy to! And let me add my hearty thanks to everyone who joins me in raising a glass! You know, we Scotsmen rarely have the opportunity to drink," he added with mock despair. The entire room laughed.

Brendan continued for several moments describing the research to determine the approximate location of the wreck, then the dives he had done to finally locate it. "There are many interesting artifacts, but before you is the most interesting I believe." He pointed to the bottle of wine on the table. "There are several bottles of this lovely Château Lafite Rothschild that have been waiting for us for well over a century. The rest will be auctioned in a few weeks, but this bottle my friends, this bottle is ours!" He waved his hands emphatically across the table, dangerous close to the bottle and the row of glasses. Dulcie inhaled sharply and put her hand on Brendan's arm.

"Thank so much, Mr. MacArthur! Next, we have another special guest, Mr. Jeremy Plunkett." Dulcie nearly hauled Brendan backwards and gestured for Jeremy to step forward. "Mr. Plunkett will be taking the Master Sommelier exam in several weeks. This honor is rare and is only available to a very few, by invitation." She turned to him. "Jeremy, can you tell us a little about this vintage, then give us your expert opinion?"

Jeremy stepped forward. This was a defining moment for him. The people in this room were wealthy, influential. If he made an impression, it could lead to much greater things. He picked up the bottle, decrepit looking after years underwater. "It looks quite ugly now, doesn't it?" Low laughter rippled throughout he group. "This wine was from a difficult year. Winters had been cold leading up to it, and France had been suffering hugely from a great wine blight caused by a tiny aphid. Half of the grapes had been destroyed. We are lucky to have this wine in front of us because it is a survivor for many reasons. First, the grapes that were used survived the blight. Second, it survived the crossing of the Atlantic. And third, it survived a shipwreck and remained well cared for at the bottom of the ocean. The ocean actually provides an excellent environment for aging wine. It's the right temperature, can oscillate the bottle gently and, in some cases, a bit of saltwater can reach the wine through osmosis and actually help to balance the flavors. So, speaking of flavors and without further ado," he glanced at Dulcie.

Brendan was supposed to pour the wine but she wasn't taking any chances. She quickly nodded and Jeremy expertly poured a small amount into a glass. He held it up to the light and began describing its color, then placed it under his nose and inhaled, describing the scents. Finally, he drank. His mouth went through several contortions that Dulcie knew were typical of a professional wine taster. The group in the room was so silent that they could hear the liquid swishing around in Jeremy's mouth.

At last he swallowed. And hesitated. Then he looked up at the group dramatically. "Surely one of the better Lafites I've tasted recently," he said simply. That was all. He put down the glass.

Brendan had expected more. "*Good God Man!* Is that all?" he boomed. The room stared at Jeremy.

Dulcie jumped forward. "Ultimately, Jeremy is a man of few words," she smiled winningly to cover her unease. "His endorsement is all that we need!" she exclaimed. "Shall we all try?" She began pouring small amounts into the little glasses and the waiter distributed them. Some guests took tiny sips at first while others downed the entire glass in one gulp. They all nodded and smiled as they talked excitedly. This was a moment for them to savor in many ways. Several asked for more. Dulcie heard Brendan say, "You can have more certainly! Just get in touch with me for the auction details! Then you can have the lot of it!"

Dulcie cringed. She had seen Dan slip into the room as Jeremy was carrying out the official tasting. He was watching Brendan. As if reading Dulcie's mind, he immediately went to Brendan's side, distracted him and led him toward the door.

Samantha was standing just inside the doorway. Brendan now sidled up to her. "Ah, this is a bonnie lassie now, is she not?" Samantha side stepped along the wall to avoid Brendan's reach. Dan continued to steer him out the door.

"This is fun," Rachel quipped from behind Dulcie.

"I'm holding my breath Rachel. We need to get everyone back downstairs. I feel as though a disaster is waiting to…," she was interrupted by a screech.

"Get *away* from me! Who do you think you are? First you drop me from your life, then you're stalking me?" Samantha was nearly screaming at Patrick Spratt. Patrick's face was bright red. "I've *seen* you outside my apartment, on the street, you creep! Don't deny it!" she added.

Patrick didn't know what to do. He was embarrassed beyond anything he had ever experienced. The entire room now stared at him.

Uncle Geoffrey began to laugh heartily. "Leave it to these young ones to provide a bit of unscheduled entertainment! We all know how celebrities love the limelight. Any limelight!" He jutted his chin in Samantha's direction.

Samantha was now speechless. Her anger extended form Jeremy to Patrick to his Uncle Geoffrey to Brendan…. She looked over at Jeremy who hung back in the room. *'No words of support. No acknowledgement that I'm his wife!'*

"Wow, you were right!" Dulcie heard Rachel whisper. Dan and Brendan had stopped in the doorway and stood there, blocking the exit. Dulcie now walked toward them, forcing them to move. Several others quietly slipped out. Dulcie saw Nick move forward and begin talking to some of the others about the wine as he artfully guided them toward the door.

Everyone had finally filtered back downstairs except for Samantha and Jeremy. "Why didn't you defend me?" she spat at him. "You let me stand there and be humiliated!"

Dulcie stood outside the room, unsure what she should do. They clearly didn't know she was there.

"I'm sick of our lives revolving around your career! I'm sick of the talk about wine all the time!" Samantha continued. "I'm sick of you!"

Dulcie heard her stomp toward the door and quickly ducked around the corner. Angry footsteps marched down the stairs.

Dulcie quietly entered the room again. Jeremy was still standing there. Dulcie expected him to look distraught. He did not. Instead, he was holding the wine bottle. He eyed the top closely, then sniffed it. He attempted to pour anything that was left into a glass, but only a bit of sediment came out. He shook his head.

Dulcie cleared her throat. Jeremy looked up at her. "I'm sorry about all of that," he said. "I think it's been brewing for a long time."

"It seems like it," Dulcie answered. "Should you get her home?"

"I would, but a couple of the people here said that they wanted to talk with me. They could be good connections for work after I pass my exam."

Dulcie was taken aback by his obvious disinterest in his wife, or in assisting Dulcie with what might continue to be a difficult situation.

Jeremy suddenly realized what Dulcie had been implying. "I'll head back down now and make sure she's simmered down. And I'll get her in a taxi home."

Dulcie couldn't think of anything to say. She nodded and followed him back downstairs knowing that the evening did indeed qualify as a disaster. The question was, just how much of a disaster was it?

The world of reality has its limits;
the world of imagination is boundless.
~ Jean-Jacques Rousseau

CHAPTER SIX

He yawned widely and peered out into the darkness. No lights were on around him, only the eerie glow of the instrument panels. The sun hadn't quite crept up over the horizon yet. In the east, he could see a vague dull blue color. In the west it was still black.

He reached around behind him and, without looking, located his thermos. Popping off the plastic cup from the top he set it down beside the instruments so that he could see into it. He couldn't turn on a light. His eyes would no longer be adjusted to the darkness. He unscrewed the insulated lid. A cloud of steam escaped as he poured coffee into the cup.

Thermos coffee. He couldn't say that he enjoyed it, but it did the trick. He always had cream and sugar in his coffee, but thermos coffee was different. He'd learned to drink it black. It was too much trouble to carry the extra items with him, and somehow it never tasted right when he added them directly to the thermos with the brew, two hours earlier while still in the warmth of his kitchen. Maybe it was because they sat mixed together for so long.

He gulped down the first cup, wishing he could be sitting at his kitchen table right now in his bathrobe and slippers rather than clomping around in heavy boots and a jacket on the bridge of an icebreaker. "It pays the bills, though," he murmured out loud. "It pays the bills."

The deckhand opened the door and a blast of cold air entered. "Hey Chuck. Ready to fire 'em up?" he asked.

"Ready as I'll ever be," Chuck quipped. He turned on the engine and heard the loud motor begin to crank. It wasn't happy about the cold, either.

The light was creeping up over the horizon. Chuck had always been surprised by how quickly it seemed to move. You couldn't see the Earth turning, but you sure could see the sun coming up. It was kind of strange. It reminded him to keep moving and get things done because that sun was going to go down just as fast.

He waited for the engines to warm, then sounded a quick blast on the horn. He always hated doing that so early in the morning. Portland was a small city, and people lived right near the harbor. He surely woke up one or two, but knew he had to. Once the big vessel began moving, anyone in the way would have to just watch out. He wasn't exactly able to stop on a dime.

He eased the bow out into the harbor, crunching through the first sheets of ice. The overnight temperature had been in negative digits. Today they would barely break zero. Cold didn't even begin to describe it.

The door opened again with another gust of freezing air. The same man who had spoken to Chuck earlier jumped inside and shut it quickly. "Man! Cold enough to freeze yer …"

"Got the gist, Conrad," Chuck said, interrupting him. He wasn't above the typical curses of a sailor, but preferred to at least start the day without swearing too much. He found himself slipping into it all too quickly as it was.

Conrad just grinned. They had worked together for quite a long time. He liked to goad his friend a little. The day was rapidly growing brighter and he peered out across the ice covered bay. "Seems kinda a shame to mess it all up sometimes, doncha think?"

Chuck snorted and smiled ruefully. "Yep. Seems like we otta leave well-enuf alone." They were silent for a moment. Chuck was staring straight ahead, carefully guiding the vessel. Conrad looked off to the port side where the docks of the city extended out into the sheets of ice. "Never seen it this bad before," he nearly whispered.

As he gazed out he saw a dark lump. "Hey, that a seal?" he said. "How the heck can they stay warm in this weather? I know they got blubber and all, but still…"

Chuck looked over. Something was strange. He'd never seen a seal just lying on the ice all on its own. He was considering calling the animal rescue people when Conrad interrupted his thoughts.

"Chuck, you think that's a seal? I mean, has to be, right? But sure don't look like one now that we're gettin' closer." A hint of anxiety had crept into Conrad's voice.

Chuck threw the engine into neutral. The ship drifted forward only slightly until it was caught in the ice ahead of it. He reached under the instrument panel and found his binoculars. He had to adjust them twice, mostly to be sure of what he was seeing. He felt a knot twist in his stomach.

"Conrad, get on the radio. Call marine patrol, or 911… both actually. That's no seal. That's a person!"

❦

Nick heard a grunt from behind him. "Any chance he's still alive?" Johnson rasped in the frigid early morning air while stomping his feet.

Nick was flattened out on the dock, peering over the edge at the body on the ice below. He twisted around and looked up at his partner. "What do you think?"

Johnson continued to stomp, shifting his hefty weight back and forth.

"And can you stop that please? It's bad enough lying here on this frozen dock without you jumping on the planks underneath me."

Johnson stopped, unfazed. "You should get up. You'll freeze to death if you stay there much longer." A marine patrol boat was approaching as closely as it could between the floating sheets of ice. "Figures it'd be low tide, eh?" he said to Nick. "Can't reach him from here."

Nick stood up and brushed off the snow from his front side. "Yeah. I know." He pulled his hat down farther over his ears. In the cold, still air he could easily hear the boat crew talking with each other. Two were in full dry suits, ready to jump in the freezing water if necessary. Two more held ropes and long gaff hooks. The boat was steered carefully around the sheet of ice.

"I see the problem," Johnson said, rubbing his hands together. "One false move and they tip that sheet. Then our body goes rolling into the drink!"

In spite of himself, Nick had to smirk. Johnson had a way with words, but he was right.

"Think it was some drunk who tripped and fell last night?" Johnson wondered. "Seems most likely.

"Probably," Nick answered. Still, he had an uneasy feeling. The clothes didn't look like those typically worn by someone on a simple drinking binge. From his vantage point he could see what appeared to be a well-tailored overcoat.

The crew below them had managed to pull the body closer across the ice, which had mercifully remained flat and intact. Nick heard someone count to three, and they hauled the body in. It was frozen in one, solid piece.

"We got pictures, yeah?" Johnson asked.

"Yep. Photographer's come and gone. I gave her the ok. She can get the rest inside when we get the body back to the morgue."

Johnson nodded. "Usually hate the morgue. Too cold. It's gonna feel like Florida in the springtime today, though," he chortled.

Nick was too cold to laugh. "Grab a coffee and head back there?" he asked.

"Yeah. What time is it?" Johnson asked.

"Don't know. I'm not pulling up my sleeve to look at my watch right now either," Nick replied.

"No matter. But hey, you know what?" Johnson was rubbing his gloved hands together again.

"What?" Nick looked at him warily.

"Standing in this cold, bet I burned off like a hundred extra calories! So you know what that means?"

Nick groaned.

"Roasters has those new cinnamon buns!"

Nick just shook his head. Johnson's thoughts almost always began and ended with his stomach.

Half an hour later the two men walked into the morgue with coffees in hand and unfastened their coats. The body they'd previously seen on the ice was lying on a table. "All right, doc, whddya got?" Johnson asked.

They walked over to the body. Johnson looked more closely. He knew this man. How did he…? "Nick, this is the guy from last night! The one who did the wine thing, remember?"

Nick had been looking at the man's hands. He quickly looked up at his face. "Damn, Johnson. I think you're right." He turned to the doctor. "Do we have an ID?"

She nodded. "Jeremy Plunkett. Lives here in Portland. We haven't notified next of kin yet though. You guys can do the honors."

Nick groaned and looked at Johnson. "Huh-uh!" he replied simply, shaking his head.

"Why do I always have to do it?" Nick lamented.

"Because you're good at it," Johnson answered. "And I have seniority."

"Well somebody has to do it, and it won't be me," the doctor chimed in. "Sorry, boys!" She turned to the body. "But you would be interested to know a couple of things first." She attempted to roll the man's head to one side slightly. "I thought this was a bump on the head that he could have received if he'd just fallen on the dock then rolled off onto the ice. But look," her finger tapped a spot on his scalp. Both men knelt down to see where she was pointing under the man's head. "We have some multiple contusions."

"So he fell more than once?" Nick asked, looking up at her.

The doctor shook her head. "I don't think so. They aren't that pronounced. What they look like is smaller bumps. Maybe from being dragged along an uneven surface, bump bump bump..." she put her hand behind her head and jerked her head back and forth on it to demonstrate.

"An uneven surface, like the planks on a frozen dock," Nick considered as he stood again. Johnson grunted as he pulled himself up, using the table for support.

"You're the detectives. I just tell you what I see," the doctor joked. "But there are a couple of other things. He's got a bruise on his wrist here, as though someone grabbed it and held it tightly. And, there was a piece of broken glass in his collar." She handed a plastic bag to Johnson. A small piece of thick green glass was in it.

"Huh," Johnson replied.

"That's all I can tell you for now. We'll have to let him thaw out a little before I can get to the rest.

Nick grimaced and nodded. "We'll stop by this afternoon," he said as he and Johnson headed for the door.

"Looking forward to it!" the doctor called from behind them.

When they stepped into the hallway Johnson nudged his partner on the shoulder. "She thinks your cute," he teased.

"Shut up," Nick answered.

"Just sayin'! It's going around the station now that you're available!"

"Does no one realize that I'm seeing someone?"

"Yeah, they don't care. Early stages. That could go awry any day, as far as they care."

"Who is 'they'?" Nick sputtered.

"All the single ladies," his partner jested. "All the single ladies, my friend!" He continued down the hallway.

Nick frowned from behind him. His mind turned to more serious matters. He would have to contact the wife, that weather girl. 'Weather forecaster,' he corrected himself. That wouldn't be easy. He caught up with Johnson.

"I'm thinking I might call Dulcie and see if she knows anything about this guy or his wife. I'll have to tell the wife soon, but I don't want to go in without at least a little more background."

"Good idea," Johnson said. He was serious now. "Wonder when exactly it happened?"

"We probably won't ever know, not with the body half frozen. Dulcie might know when he left last night, though."

"True." Johnson looked at his watch. "Bet she's at work now. Want to go over there?"

"Yeah let's. Sooner the better." They both turned around and went back through the hallway, zipping up the coats that they had yet to even remove. The cold hit them like a wall when they stepped outside.

Nick sunk his chin down into the collar of his jacket. "What'd you think of that piece of glass?" he asked Johnson.

His partner shrugged. "Could have gotten in there while someone dragged him along?"

"Maybe. What if someone hit him with a bottle and it broke?" Nick asked.

Johnson stopped quickly. "If that's the case, there'd be pieces of a broken bottle around, I would think." As he spoke, it began to snow. It was as though the clouds had burst and decided to dump as much of the powdery white flakes on them as possible. "Great," Johnson huffed, his breath coming out in a large cloud. "Now we have an excellent chance of finding it," he said sarcastically.

"Let's have a quick look on that dock though, just in case," Nick said, although he wasn't hopeful.

They hurried toward the dock where they had started their morning and kicked at the swiftly gathering snow around them as they walked up and down along it.

"Nuthin'," Johnson announced unnecessarily.

"Yep," Nick answered.

The Maine Museum of Art was located on the waterfront near the dock where they now stood. They both looked over at it. "Yeah, let's get inside," Johnson agreed to Nick's questioning look.

Nick and his partner sat in chairs facing Dulcie's desk. Their various layers of coats, hats, gloves, scarves, were scattered on the thick rug around them. They both looked very serious.

"Okay you guys are scaring me. What's going on?" Dulcie demanded. "I saw you both out there walking up and down that dock, so you can't tell me that something isn't up," she added.

Nick took a deep breath. "Yeah, something's up, Dulcie. It seems that your sommelier from last night, Jeremy Plunkett, didn't make it home."

Dulcie looked dumfounded.

"They found him on the ice in the harbor this morning," Johnson added.

That seemed to break the spell over Dulcie. She shook her head quickly as though something in it was rattling. "What?!" was all that she could say.

Both men began talking at once. Dulcie held up her hand to stop them. "Wait. Yes, I heard you. Both of you." She put her hand down. "What happened? Did he fall?"

Nick tilted his head sideways. "Sort of. Well, yes he did, but it seems that he might have been hit on the head first."

"Then dragged down the dock by his feet," Johnson added.

Dulcie stood quickly and paced around the room. She stopped and turned to them. "Does his wife know?"

Nick shook his head. "Not yet. I have to go tell her. We were hoping to get a little more information about the two of them from you first."

Dulcie returned to her desk and sat down, exhaling loudly. "I don't know very much," she said. "My friend Veronica owns the wine bar over on Middle Street. I asked her if she knew of anyone who could be our guest taster. I knew she had professional sommeliers working there from time to time. She told me about Jeremy, who was perfect. He was about to take the highest level exam in the industry. I spoke with him only once before the event last night, but it was mostly just to confirm the date and time, and for me to make sure he was right for the job, which he was."

"And his wife?" Johnson asked. "She's that weather girl, right?"

"Weather forecaster," Dulcie and Nick said simultaneously. Johnson looked back and forth between them.

"Yes, she is," Dulcie said, avoiding the term. "Samantha Sanders. I actually met her at a shop down the street by accident a couple of days ago. We were both looking for dresses to wear last night."

"And they were both quite fetching as I recall," Johnson said gallantly.

Dulcie smiled in spite of herself. "Thank you, sir."

Johnson looked smugly at Nick, who simply rolled his eyes in return.

"Hang on, though. Wouldn't Samantha be wondering where her husband is? Has she contacted the police already?" Dulcie wondered.

"Not to our knowledge," Nick said.

"Yeah, I called the station and asked them to let us know if they found out anything," Johnson added

Nick pulled out his cell phone. "Nope. Nothing."

"Still, she must be frantic by now," Dulcie insisted.

"You're right. We have to get over there. Dulcie, is there anything else you can tell us? Any impressions? General thoughts?" Nick asked.

Dulcie closed her eyes for a moment. "Samantha was clearly bothered by someone else there. The man that she shrieked at up in the board room – Patrick Spratt. She had seen him downstairs and seemed almost afraid of him. That's all I can think of," she paused for a moment. "Wait, one more thing although it may just be my interpretation and nothing more."

"We'll take if for what it's worth," Johnson said encouragingly.

"Well, when Samantha spoke about her husband, she seemed... annoyed is the only word I can think of."

Both men chuckled at the same time. "Show me a wife that isn't annoyed at her husband at one point or another?" Johnson said rhetorically.

Dulcie looked pointedly at both of them, her gaze shifting steadily to Nick. "I wouldn't know," she said flatly. "I've never been married."

Nick looked at the floor quickly. He'd hoped they'd gotten past that. Clearly they hadn't entirely.

Dulcie felt a little ashamed. The words had just come tumbling out. It wasn't entirely fair to Nick. No one could change their own past. Her face softened.

"Do you want me to come with you when you break the news to Samantha?"

Nick did, but he didn't want to risk her ire again, either. He was relieved when Johnson spoke.

"It might not be a bad idea. She might say things with you there that she wouldn't around a couple of strangers. Police-type strangers at that. Tends to make people clam up a little."

"All right then. Start suiting up," she pointed to the jackets on the floor around them, "and I'll get my coat."

ℭℬ

Samantha had been circling the coffee table in the living room for at least five minutes. She'd awakened at eight that morning to find Jeremy gone. It wasn't unusual, as sometimes he would be away all night studying with some of his wine buddies, as they called themselves. She waited until nine o'clock to call them. One by one, they all said that they had not seen him. It was nine-thirty now.

There was a knock at the door. She stopped quickly and smacked her shin against the coffee table. Wincing from the pain she limped over to the door.

"Who is it?" she asked.

Silence for a moment. Then she heard, "It's Dulcie, form the museum, and a couple of friends. Can we see you for a moment?"

Samantha's brow knitted as she opened the door. She saw the two men standing behind Dulcie. She looked at them questioningly.

"This is Nicholas Black and Adam Johnson. They were at the event last night. You might have seen them?"

Samantha nodded. "I did, but I thought you guys were security or something," she said.

Dulcie decided to get to the point. "No, but they are with the police. They're detectives. Samantha, I'm afraid we have some bad news. Can we come in?"

Samantha stepped away from the door. She gestured toward the living room. The other three looked down at their snowy boots.

"Don't be concerned about that," Samantha said. "I have a feeling it's the least of my worries right now."

They stomped off as much snow as possible and followed her into the living room. Johnson perched on the edge of a rocker trying to keep it from moving while Nick pulled a chair around from the dining table nearby. Dulcie sat on the couch with Samantha.

"What's happened," she asked.

Dulcie looked at Nick. It was his job, after all.

He cleared his throat. "I'm very sorry to tell you Ms. Plunkett,"

"Sanders," she corrected.

"Yes, I'm sorry. Ms. Sanders. Your husband was found dead this morning. It appears that he was hit or fell at some time during the night."

Samantha quickly stood and began pacing around the coffee table again. Dulcie had to pull her legs to the side quickly to avoid Samantha's stride. "Where?" she interjected, still walking.

"Where was he found?" Nick asked. He was watching her intently. She nodded. "He was on an ice sheet in the harbor beneath a dock very close to the museum."

Samantha nodded again, still circling.

"Did your husband come home with you last night?" Johnson now spoke up.

Samantha shook her head, still circling. Dulcie put out a hand and stopped her. Samantha bumped into it and looked startled. "Can you sit for a minute?" Dulcie asked.

Samantha sat down beside Dulcie. "I knew something was wrong. I knew it! I knew it! I knew it!" she kept repeating the last words.

Dulcie decided to keep talking. "When I spoke with Jeremy last, he said that he was going to get you a cab home. Did that happen?" she asked.

Samantha suddenly fell back into the couch. It was as though she had just deflated. "Yes," she said flatly.

"And that's the last you saw of him?" Nick added.

"Yes," she repeated.

"All right," Dulcie said. "Is there anything I can do for you? Someone I could call?"

"My mother," Samantha said. She didn't move.

Dulcie glanced around the room for a phone. Johnson spotted it on the table near him and handed it to her.

"Can you leave now please?" It wasn't a request. Samantha's tone was adamant.

Dulcie eyed her for a moment, then stood. "Of course," she said. "This is a shock. I'm sure if these gentlemen have any more questions, they can get in touch with you."

"Yes," Samantha replied quietly.

The three visitors trooped out the door. As Dulcie closed it behind her she could have sworn she heard Samantha sigh. It sounded like a sigh of relief.

They hesitated by the door until they could vaguely hear Samantha talking on the phone. Only then did they quietly make their way onto the street again. The snow was coming down harder now.

"Not a chance we'll find any of that broken bottle now," Johnson muttered.

"If there's any to be found," Nick countered.

"What bottle?" Dulcie asked.

Both men stopped. They'd forgotten how little they had told her. "Coroner found a piece of glass in Jeremy's shirt collar. Looks like it might have come from a bottle. Green. He could have been hit on the head with one, or it might have just gotten caught under his collar when he was dragged."

They continued walking again. It was too cold to stand in one place. "That's interesting," Dulcie said. "But how do you know he was dragged? Maybe he was out on the dock and just fell over?"

"Don't think so," Nick said. "The coroner said that he had multiple contusions on his head. Bruises."

"I know what a contusion is," Dulcie interjected.

"Okay, sorry. Just don't want to do too much of the police lingo. Could get annoying," he replied.

'*Is this a reference to that earlier conversation about wives being annoyed with their husbands?*' Dulcie thought. '*Because we're a long way from that, yet.*' She frowned. "Multiple contusions…," she repeated, prompting him to say more.

"Yup, like his head bumped along, hitting something hard over and over a few times," Johnson chimed in.

"Like the uneven planks of a frozen dock as he was dragged along," Dulcie concluded.

"Right," Nick said.

"It's a really good theory. Make's sense," she said thoughtfully. "How did he actually die? Was it the blow to his head, or did he freeze to death?"

"Don't know," Johnson answered. "Coroner's still looking at the body. Why?"

"I was just thinking. It'd take a lot of force to hit him that hard," she said.

"Very true, unless you get lucky and hit in the right place," Nick replied.

"Jeremy isn't, I mean wasn't, a big man either, but it would still take someone fairly strong to drag him down the dock and shove his body over the edge," Dulcie added.

"And you think Samantha couldn't have done that?" Johnson asked. "You think she isn't big enough?" His chin was stuffed into his jacket collar and his voice was muffled.

"Anything's possible if you're motivated enough, I suppose," Dulcie mused.

Motivation. That's what they needed to determine, Nick thought. Why would someone be motivated to kill Jeremy Plunkett?

They reached the museum entrance. "Here's my stop, gentlemen," Dulcie announced. "I'll let you know if I think of anything."

They both nodded and turned away. Dulcie watched them trudge along. She wished Nick wasn't leaving. Her world felt out of order just now, and his presence somehow seemed to put everything back into perspective.

As if hearing her thoughts, he glanced back. She waved. She couldn't see his mouth beneath his collar, but his eyes seemed to crinkle into a smile. He waved back.

There. At least that helped a little. Dulcie quickly opened the door, entered the museum vestibule where warm air blasted on her, and stomped the snow off her boots. Why did she have the feeling that this was going to be a very long winter?

You come to nature with all her theories,
and she knocks them all flat.
~ Pierre-Auguste Renoir

CHAPTER SEVEN

Geoffrey Spratt wasn't so far removed from the origins of the family fortune that he didn't understand the requirements of maintaining it. On the contrary, he understood all too well that inheritance was only half of the game, especially when inheritance meant managing funds along with siblings and cousins. It was a tricky business.

Patrick was another story. He hadn't been a stranger to hard work, but for some reason could not grasp the concept of money management. It seemed to slip through his fingers if not exactly like water, then certainly like pudding. The result was the same. A sticky mess.

That girl he'd been with, Samantha, seemed to ground him. She was smart, practical. Geoffrey had breathed a sigh of relief when he thought things were getting serious between them. If the boy had a good wife to look after things, Geoffrey wouldn't have to worry quite so much about keeping his nephew afloat. Samantha didn't seem to be the gold-digger type, either. That was reassuring.

Then the idiot went and broke up with her. Geoffrey couldn't even talk to him for days after he'd found out. "Why?" was all he could say at the time.

"I don't know. I was getting bored," was the answer. So that's what his nephew thought life was all about. Excitement. He had a lot to learn.

Geoffrey had made it very clear that he thought Patrick had made one of the more idiotic decisions of his life. When Geoffrey finally had calmed down enough to speak to Patrick again he had explained a few things. One of them was the fact that people had to complement each other in a relationship. He pointed out how Samantha had filled in the gaps where Patrick was lacking.

Patrick had not appreciated his uncle's concern. Instead he had grown angry. "Like you would know?" he had yelled. "You've never been married!"

It was true. Geoffrey Spratt had never been in that situation. But he was a keen observer of those around him. Managing a fortune that was pooled within an extended family required a careful understanding of personalities. He made it his business to learn exactly how all of the interrelationships worked, and more importantly, how they didn't work.

Geoffrey had sighed, realizing that he would have to fall back on the last resort. He would need to financially cut Patrick loose. The manner that this was carried out, however, was critical. Geoffrey had informed his nephew that he was at the age where he would receive the first installment of a trust fund. A large sum was deposited into Patrick's back account. It was all that he would see of the family money for five years, until the next installment was released. This whole scheme was completely fabricated by Geoffrey of course, but Patrick need never know.

If Patrick had been smart, he would have invested the majority of the money. Geoffrey had hinted that he would be happy to help Patrick, to advise on solid investments, if he was interested.

Within a few months, it was clear that Patrick had no interest in investing. Curiously, he didn't seem interested in spending the money on flashy items, symbolic of the rich, either. Where the money went, Geoffrey had no idea. Patrick just spent it on whatever whim interested him at the moment. Within the first year he had managed to eliminate over half of his bank account.

Patrick himself had not actually noticed this. Not at first. It was Uncle Geoffrey who had pointed it out, indirectly. A year after the money had been handed over, Geoffrey had said, "So it's been a year that you've had your fund now Patrick. How's it going?" Of course Patrick had replied that everything was fine. But when he checked the balance he'd been shocked.

That's when he had begun to brood. He couldn't ask his uncle for advice. It would make him look like an idiot, as though he couldn't handle being an adult. He cast his thoughts back over his past and realized that for the entire time that he and Samantha had been together, she had kept things on course. For the first time, he began to at least acknowledge, if not actually appreciate, what she was capable of bringing to his life.

He knew that he needed her back. That was clear. He had been staggeringly unsuccessful in the dating world anyway. He hadn't realized how much of a catch she was until he had others to hold up in comparison. Basically, they didn't stand a chance.

The day he had turned on the television and saw the weather report was the day that he became officially obsessed. For one thing, she looked even more incredible on TV than he had remembered her to be in real life. And that was saying quite a lot. He remembered that she had always turned heads whenever they were out, no matter where they went.

She was never happy with the attention, though. Why then would she take a job on television? He had needed answers, and it wasn't long before he had pieced together what had happened in her life since he had left her. She had met someone, gone through a whirlwind romance, got married, and now essentially was supporting both of them. Thus the television job.

Patrick had known then that it was time to take action. He didn't even know Samantha's husband, but he was certain that the dolt was all wrong for her. He needed to be gone. Away. Out of the picture. And the more Patrick had thought about it, the more he had known exactly what to do.

Geoffrey knew that this husband needed to be gone as well. He had several ideas, each somewhat more unsavory than the next. However, the beauty of having a fortune at one's disposal was that the unsavory work need never fall into one's own hands. A handful of cash followed by turning one's head in the opposite direction was all that was required. As for any feelings of guilt, Geoffrey had long since learned to deal with that. He had become a master of justification. He found it very easy to justify his nephew's happiness along with his solidity within the family realm.

Unfortunately, everything had just happened too quickly. The night before had been a bit of a fiasco. Geoffrey hadn't counted on Patrick behaving like a psychopath; he hadn't known that the stupid boy was essentially stalking his former girlfriend.

Geoffrey didn't blame Samantha one bit for her reaction. Under the same circumstances, he'd probably have done the same thing. Now it was time for damage control. He needed to repair this rift and quickly.

Geoffrey sat back in his chair and put his fingertips together, almost in a praying gesture. He brought his forefingers to his lips, tapping them repeatedly. It was his thinking attitude.

It would take a lot of work now, getting her back with Patrick. She wasn't the type to be won over with overt attention either. That was so obvious to

Geoffrey. Why wasn't it obvious to Patrick? Geoffrey knew the answer to that. Patrick was only thinking about himself. He didn't give Samantha the kind of appreciation that she would want. It was all about Patrick.

Geoffrey tapped his lips several more times, then his hands froze in midair. He smiled. Maybe Samantha didn't want attention, but a few thoughtful gifts, perhaps to say "I'm sorry," never went amiss. Now what to get was the question. He'd need to think more on that one.

Meanwhile, he picked up his phone and called his nephew. The fool didn't answer. Geoffrey waited for Patrick's recorded voice to stop droning on, then said, "Patrick. It's your Uncle. We need to talk. Do not, under any circumstances, contact Samantha and for God sake, stop walking up and down her street! Call me when you get this. Or better yet, just get over here." He clicked the phone off.

Patrick sat in his living room. He had watched his phone buzz on the coffee table. It had jiggled around as it rang. He knew the number. When it stopped, he waited. He knew a message would be coming. Moments later it sounded the little chime telling him that he had voicemail. Reluctantly, he pressed the button and listen to his uncle's voice fill the room.

He was right of course. Uncle Geoffrey was always right. Patrick hung his head in his hands for several seconds, then brought them down quickly, smacking his thighs. He stood up, shoving the phone in his pocket, found his coat and left the apartment.

Outside he realized that he had forgotten his gloves. Again. He shoved his hands deep in the coat pockets. He had to remember to put an extra pair in them. Then again, he fully realized that his evening treks down the street to a certain apartment window were about to be curtailed, so why bother.

C3

Dulcie had just become absorbed in reading a new research paper and was annoyed by the knock on her door. "Yes?" she said, a bit too quickly.

Rachel opened it and poked her head in. "Do you have time for an unscheduled visitor?" she asked. Suddenly she was thrown off balance as the door was shoved open from behind her. She stumbled into Dulcie's office followed by the much larger Brendan MacArthur.

"Aye, lassie! Of course she has time!" His voice sounded like a bellow in the quiet room.

Rachel gave Dulcie a quick, very pointed look of apology and sympathy combined, and scurried out. She left the door open behind her.

Brendan grinned as she left, then closed the door. '*The nerve….*,' thought Dulcie, but then, that was one thing Brendan had always had in abundance.

"Quite a night we had, was it not?" he asked rhetorically and didn't wait for an answer. "Certainly was entertaining. I'll bet your gossips have been chattering already!"

Dulcie very slowly, and very pointedly, closed the lid of her laptop. She gestured toward the seat in front of her desk. She stared at Brendan for a moment.

This was a side of her that Brendan had never seen. He was not aware that in the years since Dulcie had left him and Oxford behind, she had worked very hard on maintaining control, whether it was of herself or those around her. She hated the feeling of everything spinning. He sat quietly for a moment, an unusual posture for him.

At last she spoke in a very low, clear voice. "Brendan. Are you aware that someone died last night?"

Brendan looked surprised. "From your stern look here lass, I'm assuming it's someone we know? I'm sure a lot of people died last night somewhere on the planet." He chuckled at his joke.

Dulcie simply nodded. She wasn't smiling.

Brendan cleared his throat. "What happened? Did one of the old codgers kick the bucket right here in the museum? Maybe it isn't so bad – they could have left a legacy for your little museum in their will."

Dulcie was beyond the point of irritation but somehow maintained her composure. "No, it was not some 'old codger' as you put it. It was someone quite young. Our sommelier, as a matter of fact. He was found this morning." She chose not to mention how or where he was found.

"No! You don't say!" Brendan exclaimed. "So young, too, as you say! Was it an accident? Or some freak medical condition perhaps?"

Dulcie felt as though Brendan was not being quite genuine with this response but she let it go. "I don't know the details," she said simply. "But I do know that it happened sometime last night. He was found this morning." For some reason she felt compelled to withhold all of the facts.

"My goodness!" Brendan said. "What a tragedy! How is his beautiful wife taking it?"

Dulcie bristled slightly when he called Samantha 'beautiful.' There was no doubt that she was, but why did he feel the need to say it just now? And why was she reacting in this stupid way? Was it a tinge of jealousy? She didn't think so. It just seemed inappropriate to mention such a thing when the poor woman's husband was suddenly dead.

"I believe she's mostly in shock, from what I understand." At that moment Dulcie remembered that Brendan had barged in without warning. Why? "Brendan, what brings you here?" she asked sharply.

He looked away with a half-smile. Dulcie realized then that she'd caught him off guard. He had forgotten how well she knew him.

"Just wanted to chat about events last night," he muttered. "But sounds like matters have taken a rather serious turn, so I'd best be off."

She said nothing as he stood.

"But there is one thing," he added. "Just if you think of it, could you jot down a few of the names of our fellow revelers? Perhaps an address or two? I think it's always best, after all, to send a proper thank you."

So that's what he wanted. Inside information. Her policy was strict on that. She shook her head. "Brendan, I'm sure you realize that I can't just go giving out names and addresses of any of our donors, let alone the wealthiest ones. Rest assured that I will be sending a thank you note to each and every one, and I will be sure to mention your thanks as well."

It was all he could do not to swear out loud. He needed to drum up interest in the wine quickly. His plan had altered. He didn't, in fact, want to send the remaining wine to auction. He wanted to sell the bottles directly, in a somewhat more clandestine fashion. It would certainly benefit everyone involved. Those pesky authorities who liked to collect taxes and such really need never know.

Regaining his composure, he said, "Of course. Stupid of me, really. Please pass on my hearty thanks, and do tell them what a pleasure it was to meet them."

"I will, Brendan." Dulcie stood now, ushering him out of her office.

As she opened the door, he leaned over and brushed her cheek with his lips. Neither of them realized that Detective Nicholas Black was standing immediately on the other side, his hand raised in a fist to knock.

Dulcie jumped back with a gasp.

Brendan looked startled, then broke out in a boisterous laugh. "Ah the long arm of the law! Quite literally, I see!"

Nick quickly lowered his arm. It was all he could do to keep it at his side and not let it spring forward, punching the smug Scottish bastard in the jaw. He turned to Dulcie. "I wanted to ask you a few questions, about what we were, um," he glanced at Brendan now, "What we were discussing earlier?"

"Ah now! Would this be the death of the young man?" Brendan interjected. "I thought there was something to that, but our lassie here was cagey!" He reached over and tousled a lock of her hair on her shoulder. "But then, she does cagey very well, wouldn't you agree?"

Seething. There was no other word for Nick's emotions at that moment. He forced a smile that did not reach his eyes. "Dulcie does a lot of things very well. Especially her job." He turned to her. "Do you have a moment?" he asked, effectively dismissing Brendan.

"Yes, I do," she answered, stepping back from the door. She nodded at Brendan. "I'll let you know when the thank-you notes have been sent. Good luck with the wine sales." She knew that Brendan would wince inwardly as she said that in front of a police detective. Brendan never did anything above board. She closed the door on Brendan as soon as Nick entered.

"You're quite chummy," Nick said quietly.

Indignation began to rise within Dulcie for at least the second time in less than twenty-four hours. What was it about the presence of these two men in the same room that made her so annoyed? The fact that they each seemed to lay claim to her, as though she were simply a piece of chattel? Some women may enjoy that sort of thing, but she was not one of them.

"I'll ignore that comment," she bristled. "Brendan and I have a past. You do as well, as I recall." The words slipped out before she could stop them.

"Yes, but my past is just that. Past. I have had no direct contact for years," he retorted.

"Nor have I until that hulk simply reappeared. Short of being completely rude and unappreciative of his generous gift, what am I supposed to do?"

"Oh please, Dulcie! You know as well as I do that he didn't give you that wine as a gift. It was a sales pitch. A marketing tool. He's going to sell most of that wine illegally, under the table, to the people in that boardroom last night!" Nick couldn't stop himself. He was angry that Brendan MacArthur had reappeared in Dulcie's life when they were just kindling a relationship and establishing trust.

"What bothers you more, the fact that he's selling antiquities illegally or the fact that he's flirting with me?" There. She'd said it.

"Both, now that you mention it!" he stammered.

Dulcie shook her head and walked back to her desk. "Did you want to talk about something, Nick? I mean, other than this?" she asked pointedly.

Nick just shook his head. "I did, but it can wait. I mostly just wanted to make sure that you were okay, but I can see that you are."

"Look Nick, I didn't invite him here," Dulcie began.

"No," Nick interjected. "Let's just stop. We're not making any sense and to be honest, I can't think straight right now."

Dulcie exhaled forcefully. She felt the same way but she wasn't going to admit it. "All right. We both probably have too much on our minds right now. Do you want to get together for coffee later?"

Nick visibly relaxed. He felt the knots in his back easing away. "Yes. Yes I do. That's a great idea. Can you call me when you have time?"

Dulcie nodded and found herself fully exhaling for the first time since he had come in the room. "I will," she said simply.

Nick gave her a serious look, then left, closing the door quietly behind him.

"Men!" Dulcie said out loud once he was gone, shaking her head vigorously. But in this case it was only one man that was the problem. Nothing had gone right since Brendan MacArthur had walked back into her life.

◌

Samantha had called her mother, but it would take at least an hour for her to arrive. As soon as she had put down the phone she'd gone into the bathroom splashed cold water on her face for several minutes, then pulled her hair back into a tight ponytail. She stared at herself in the mirror.

What the hell had she done? Why had she married him in the first place? How could she have let her life spin so far out of control like this? She had no idea what was happening anymore.

She walked slowly into the kitchen. Tea. That's what she needed. A strong cup of tea. She filled the electric kettle and switched it on, then scrounged through the cupboard for a box of teabags. Some of Jeremy's unopened wine bottles clanked against each other. Samantha froze, startled by the sound.

She took the first one down and gently placed it on the counter. She set the second down a bit more forcefully. The third slammed on to the Formica, followed by the fourth, fifth, sixth... She yanked open a drawer, pulled out a corkscrew and shoved it into the top of the nearest bottle. The cork came out more easily than she anticipated sending her backwards and nearly sloshing wine on her shirt. She lunged forward again, held the bottle upside-down over the sink and watched the wine glug out onto the stainless steel and swirl down the drain. She turned on the faucet, then repeated the process with every single bottle. She even went through the other cupboards locating more.

By the time the kettle had reached a boil, Samantha had managed to empty twenty bottles. She poured hot water over the teabag and, while waiting for it to steep, put the bottles into neat, orderly rows. They looked like soldiers, rank and file. Dead soldiers. It was all gone and it wasn't coming back.

*The emotions are sometimes so strong
that I work without knowing it.
The strokes come like speech.*

~ Vincent van Gogh

CHAPTER EIGHT

"Blow to the head," the doctor said. "That's what knocked him out. The blow to the head. But I don't think that's what killed him. More likely he died of exposure. It wouldn't take long with these temperatures we've been having."

Nick glanced down at the sheet that covered the body of Jeremy Plunkett. It looked cold. Everything in the room was cold. Nick felt like the whole world had gone cold.

Evidently, the doctor did not. She stepped closer to Nick, eyeing him coyly. "How's the investigating going, detective?" She said. "I'd be happy to help if you need to go over any case notes." She batted her eyelashes at him.

Either Nick didn't notice her overt attempt at flirtation, or he concealed his response well. He simply pulled out his notebook, flipped through it, then put it back in his pocket.

"No other pieces of glass or anything on him?" Nick asked.

The doctor let out a decided huff before replying, "Nothing else." She stepped back away from Nick.

Johnson tried not to grin at the spectacle. He'd been noticing a lot more women paying attention to Nick. When he'd first joined the force the rumors had been that his preference was not for women, but that was before the whisperings about his recent divorce. No one had known he'd been married. Of course the fact that Nick already seemed to be favoring someone new was of little consequence. "All's fair!" as many of them said.

"Okay, thanks Christina. I think we're done here," Nick said without looking at her.

She turned without saying a word and went back into her office.

"Nuthin' like a little lust over a stiff," Johnson quipped. "Body, I mean."

Nick rolled his eyes. "Really, Johnson. There wasn't any…"

Johnson chuckled under his breath. "Save it. There was. You're just too dense to notice."

Nick was instantly reminded of the argument he had had with Dulcie. "I'm starting to think that women are more trouble than they're worth."

"Spoken like a man who's been screwed over in the past," Johnson observed. "But I thought it was going well now with Dulcie. What's up? Not that brutish boyfriend back in town?" He smirked at his alliteration.

"Ex-boyfriend," Nick corrected. He glanced toward Christina's office, then nodded toward the morgue door. "Let's get a coffee. I'm freezing."

They wound through the corridor then out the front door. Both men zipped up their jackets and pulled out knit hats and gloves from their pockets, jamming them on as quickly as they could.

"Holy Jesus, it takes your breath away, doesn't it. And not in a good way," Johnson complained.

"Yeah. Remind me why we live here?" Nick replied, his voice muffled by his collar. They tramped down the street at a steady clip. Johnson's breath heaved in great white clouds as they finally reached their 'other office' as they called it, the coffee shop Roasters.

They gave their order at the counter then found a booth. Johnson preferred the booths. He didn't like how 'spindly' the chairs looked, as he put it.

"Okay, so first things first, then we'll get down to business. What's up with you and Dulcie. I'm sensing tension," Johnson said as he pulled off his hat. What was left of his hair now topped his head in a messy swirl. Johnson dragged a quick hand through it which did nothing to help.

"Nick left his hat on. He hunkered down more on the seat. "Yeah, you could say that," he muttered.

"And…" Johnson prompted.

Nick sighed and shook his head. "It was stupid, really. I went over to talk with her about our dead guy since she knew him. I had just reached her door when the slimy Scotsman was leaving and I saw him kiss her."

Johnson's eyebrows shot up. "Really? Right on the smacker?"

Nick frowned. "No, on the cheek."

Johnson leaned across the table and whacked his partner on the forehead. "You got sore because he kissed her on the cheek?"

Nick simply nodded.

"Well then, let's break this down. First, the guy is an old boyfriend, so they knew each other well, probably in the Biblical sen…,"

"Don't need to mention that," Nick interjected.

"Oh. Sorry. Well moving right along… Second, he's from another country with different customs."

"I've never heard of the Scottish people as a whole being overwhelmingly affectionate," Nick countered.

Johnson paid no attention to him. "And third, what was Dulcie's reaction to it? Was she annoyed or didn't she seem to mind?"

Nick thought for a moment. "Now that you mention it, she seemed annoyed. But then she could have been annoyed just because I showed up at an inopportune moment."

Johnson reached out to smack his partner again but Nick dodged out of the way this time.

"I thought I had trained you better than this," Johnson announced to the universe at large. "Let's cast our minds back, shall we? I recall that at a certain event which happened *only last night* our girl Dulcie was annoyed, perhaps even concerned, with the so-called slimy Scotsman. In fact, she requested and received our assistance to keep him under control. Does that sound like someone that she's warming up to again, after all these years?"

Nick was silent.

"Now I want you to think very carefully," Johnson continued. "When the aforementioned kiss on the cheek was taking place, what exactly did Dulcie do? Did she stretch up to him? Lean in?"

"Um, well, not really…" Nick stammered.

Johnson sat back and took a tentative sip of coffee. "I rest my case," he concluded.

Nick felt ashamed that he had assumed Dulcie was welcoming her old boyfriend's advances. He suddenly felt very embarrassed as well. "I suppose it's just a case of old-fashioned jealousy," he admitted.

"I'd say so," Johnson said, eyeing the pastries behind the counter longingly. He sighed heavily and turned back to Nick. "Think you might owe her a small apology?" he said.

"Probably a big one," Nick replied. "What's the name of that flower shop across the street from the museum?" he asked.

Johnson grinned. "Good man!" Then he shrugged his shoulders. "Don't remember. You'll have to look it up."

Nick nodded. "All right. Well. Now that that's settled, there's the other matter of the body in the morgue. Any thoughts?"

Johnson put down his coffee cup. "Seemed a respectable type from what we know, which isn't much. Someone may have had a grudge."

"It wasn't a mugging or they'd have taken his wallet," Nick replied. "Something tells me that it had to be someone at that party. Trouble is, I don't think that many people actually knew him."

"No, but they sure knew his wife," Johnson mused. "Think she's worth killing for?"

It was a good question. Nick thought for a moment. Would he kill to have Dulcie? No, that was ridiculous. But he would certainly fight for her. He remembered how hotheaded he had felt earlier when he saw her with Brendan. Even a sane person able to maintain moderate self-control most of the time could snap. Was that what had happened? Had someone confronted Jeremy Plunkett and snapped, hitting him on the head? Then could they have panicked, dragged him down the dock, and rolled him onto the ice below?

"You're thinking what I'm thinking," Johnson said eyeing his partner intently. "Furthermore, think about the timeframe. He was found early this morning when it was low tide. When our killer did their work, it would have been high tide. Maybe they thought the body would float away in an ice sheet in the meantime when the tide went out? It's about a ten foot difference between high and low. That's a lot of water moving around."

"Yeah, but the ice. It was just packed in. Even if the water is moving around, the ice hasn't been very much," Nick protested.

"True, but it seemed more like a spur-of-the-moment hot-headed kind of murder. Whoever it was probably wasn't really thinking about the ice," Johnson replied. "Or maybe they were thinking about it but they just weren't much of an oceanographer or meteorologist or whatever those scientists are that study that stuff."

Both men looked at each other, a thought dawning on them at the same instant.

"Didn't that weather girl go home early?" Johnson asked.

"Forecaster," Nick corrected.

"Huh?" Johnson was confused.

"Weather forecaster. And yes, she did," he said quietly. "Yes she did," he added without realizing that he was still speaking out loud.

&

Brendan MacArthur paced. He was not a pacer, typically. But now he found himself walking up and down the length of his hotel room. He growled softly.

Everything had been going so well, then Dulcie had to ruin it. It just figured that her damned boyfriend was a police detective. That's the last thing Brendan needed.

He had wanted to use her, or more to the point, her connections, to drum up interest in the wine. Free marketing. He didn't want anything to be high profile. He'd told everyone that he was going to auction the rest of the bottles, but had never registered them with an auction house. He had no intention of doing that – it would have brought everything to the attention of the authorities and he wanted this to be a nice, relatively quiet underground transaction. Most of the buyers would have wanted that too, he knew from experience.

He'd had a few calls from people interested, but they had all led to the inevitable question: which auction house was handling the sale? If Brendan had managed to keep everything low-profile, that question would never have been asked. They would have suggested an "arrangement" on the spot. He knew his clientele.

Fortunately, Brendan had never said how many bottles he had. He doubted the others on the dive team knew. Brendan had made sure to keep the crates closed.

Maybe he could still sell some on the side to a few brave souls who dared? He thought about the tasting in the boardroom. Who was there? Brendan was annoyed that Dulcie hadn't given him the guest list. Still, he did remember a few names. He hadn't been as drunk as others may have thought. It was part of the act, something that he'd learned long ago. Pretend you're a bit drunk and not only can you get away with asking things that you couldn't otherwise, but you can also get others to talk more too. Most people want to tell their secrets, and they're far more willing if they don't think you'll remember them the next morning.

Brendan went over to the desk and opened his laptop. He tapped in the few names that he remembered. Then a thought occurred to him: the big donors would probably be on the board of directors, too. With any luck, there would be pictures of each one.

Brendan went to the museum's web site and quickly found the board list. He grinned. There they were. Quite a few familiar faces. He quickly started taking notes.

An hour later, Brendan sat back and closed the computer. The next step was crucial. He couldn't exactly call each person and ask if they wanted to buy the wine. He'd have to figure out a way to rub shoulders with them. This was the tricky bit and now, with recent events, time was of the essence. He stood and started pacing around the room again.

☙

Dulcie was already aggravated, and now this. She whirled around, her eyes piercing through Rachel. "You mean to tell me that we have to close the exhibit until we get a motion sensor installed?"

Rachel stood very calmly in front of her boss. "I don't *mean* to tell you. I *am* telling you," she said calmly. "And don't shoot the messenger!" she added.

Dulcie collapsed into her chair. "Why didn't we know about this before?"

Rachel sat down in the chair beside Dulcie's desk. "As you know, we're the first ones for this exhibit. Somebody screwed up and forgot to mention it. But it's only one painting that requires it – the museum that loaned it made the stipulation for extra security which was evidently left out of the paperwork. Until now."

"And do they have any idea what this will cost?" Dulcie exclaimed.

"One of the exhibit's national sponsors already said that they'd 'absorb' the cost. Don't you love that word? I wish someone would 'absorb' the cost of my rent," Rachel mused. She smirked, then refocused. "Anyway, cost isn't an issue right now, but time is."

Dulcie sat up straight. "Absolutely, yes it is." Her mind was whirring already. "All right, we have two options. Take down the painting until we can get a crew in here to install the system which means we can leave the rest of the exhibit open, or close the exhibit entirely and disappoint a number of people planning to see it …"

"Until we can get a crew in here to install the system," Rachel finished for her.

"Right," Dulcie agreed. She glanced up at her assistant. "Do you think this whole thing is cursed?

First the insanity of last night, then a body on the ice, and now this?"

"WHAT?!" Rachel gasped.

"Oh, that's right. You probably don't know yet. Remember our sommelier from last night? He appeared this morning out on the ice under that dock over there." She motioned with her head out the window.

Rachel squinted, stretching her neck around to look out the window. "Seriously?" was all she could say.

Dulcie nodded. "The police are keeping it quiet at the moment. It might be 'foul play' as they so quaintly call it."

"Why would someone want that guy dead? Oh, wait a minute… didn't he and his wife, that weather girl…"

"Forecaster," Dulcie interjected.

"What?" Rachel stopped.

"Nothing. Long story. Keep going," Dulcie replied.

Rachel continued. "He and his wife got in a big argument and he sent her home early. I saw the cab pull up. Do you think she could have…"

Dulcie shrugged her shoulders. "I don't know. It's pretty awful, but I don't really know any of them. All I do know is that whenever Brendan MacArthur is around, things somehow seem to get out of control. And this," she waved her hand in front of the paperwork that Rachel had put on the desk, "This is no exception."

"You can't blame Brendan for this," Rachel interjected.

"Maybe not," said Dulcie. "But it's just his aura or something. Chaos follows him like a lonely puppy."

Rachel burst out laughing. Dulcie was silent, shaking her head.

"Wait, wasn't your boyfriend in here earlier? Is that what you were talking about? The wine guy getting murdered?"

Dulcie had momentarily forgotten about Nick. Now their argument came flooding back. "Slow down. No one said anyone was murdered. But yes, Nick was in here," she replied quickly.

Rachel was about to quip about Nick's frequent visits, but one look at Dulcie made her think twice.

Dulcie quickly changed the subject. "Let's take down the painting for now and lock it up. I'll take care of that. Can you call around to see if any of the security companies can get in here pronto to set up the motion system?"

"Already done. There's one in Boston that just had a cancellation in their schedule. I asked them to tentatively hold the spot open until I'd talked with you," Rachel replied.

"Rachel, as always, you are a gem. A peach. And I can't thank you enough," Dulcie sighed with some relief. At least something was going right.

"Sure you can!" Rachel exclaimed, now standing. "In my next paycheck!" She heard Dulcie snort from behind her as she left the room.

ℂ℥

Patrick Spratt sat in his uncle's chilly West End mansion rubbing his hands briskly in front of an ineffectual fire. Uncle Geoffrey shuffled in. "Don't you heat this place?" asked Patrick without turning around.

"Course I do. One room at a time. Usually it's just me, so why the hell would I heat the whole house? Just warm up the room I'm in."

"Well you're in this room now," Patrick said.

Geoffrey went back out then came back with an electric space heater. He plugged it in to the wall outlet and turned it on. Patrick noticed that the dial was only on the medium setting.

"Uncle, you have the money to heat the entire house. Why don't you?" Patrick protested. He reached over and switched the heater to the highest setting.

Geoffrey switched it back. "I'm in charge of the family wealth, and I intend to keep us in that state. Wealthy, I mean."

"Isn't the whole point of being wealthy being comfortable?" Patrick grumbled.

Geoffrey went over to a side cupboard and pulled out a bottle of Glenmorangie. He sloshed a generous amount into two glasses. "There, that make you feel better?" he asked handing one to his nephew. Geoffrey shook his head thinking how soft the boy had become.

Patrick sat down in a leather chair near the fire. He tipped the glass back, sipping the scotch. "Ahh, thanks Uncle. This is the good stuff!"

They were silent for several minutes.

"So you've heard," Patrick said.

"Yes, I have," his uncle replied slowly.

"Do you think this changes anything?" asked Patrick.

Geoffrey gazed at his nephew. How could he be so thick sometimes? "Uh, yes my boy. This changes everything."

Patrick nodded. "She hates me. That hasn't changed."

"It can though," Geoffrey countered. "There was a time when she didn't hate you. Sometimes hate and love can flip back and forth pretty fast."

"Do you think she's worth it?" Patrick asked, peering into his glass.

"Do you?" Geoffrey knew the answer as well as Patrick did. Without Samantha as the rock in his life, Patrick drifted around pointlessly.

"What do the police know? Do they know?" Geoffrey asked rhetorically. He was referring to Patrick's evening wanderings. It was the more important question at the moment than whether or not Samantha could fall in love with Patrick again.

Patrick looked up at his uncle. "How would I know? Do you think it's a problem?"

Geoffrey closed his eyes in an effort to keep himself from saying out loud what he was thinking. *The fact that you're essentially stalking a married ex-girlfriend at night, then her husband is found dead could be considered problematic...* Patrick had never been known to be clever.

Instead, Geoffrey said, "After hearing that girl screeching last night, they're going to start asking you questions soon enough. You've got the perfect motive for wanting him dead." It was the first time either of them had said the word out loud.

Patrick had an idea. "Wouldn't that make me the least likely choice, though? I mean, on TV it's never the obvious one."

Geoffrey shook his head. "This is decidedly not TV. And you have decidedly screwed up with your actions in front of everyone last night. The police will be getting in touch with you pronto. They're probably at your apartment right now."

Patrick's hand began to shake. "Look, they can't possibly think that I did it!"

"Sure they can," Geoffrey muttered. He had to make a plan. Otherwise dear Patrick would screw up everything. Again. Geoffrey downed the rest of his scotch and set the heavy leaded crystal glass down on the coffee table in front of him with a firm thunk.

Patrick jumped. His head snapped around to look intently at his uncle. "What should I do?" he whispered.

Uncle Geoffrey stood up to locate the scotch bottle again. He brought it over to the table and refilled his glass. He didn't bother with Patrick's. He could get his own this time. Geoffrey eased back into his chair and let his gaze rest on the flames in front of him. "The first thing you'll do," he said, still watching the fire, "Is you'll move in with me. If anyone asks, you did a couple of days ago because you were worried about my health. It was before the art museum thing." He glanced up at Patrick, half expecting him to have lost focus already and start complaining about the heating situation again. To Geoffrey's surprise, Patrick was nodding, intent on every word.

"Secondly," Geoffrey continued, "You'll give me your phone. If anyone asks, you lost it someplace. I'll let the battery run out and just put it somewhere in the house. It will seem as though you dropped it when you came here and couldn't find it again. Then, if the damned police start searching places and they find it, we've got a good explanation."

"Why do we need to get rid of my phone?" asked Patrick.

"Because they're going to call you, and I don't want them to get through. We need a good reason for that. Losing your phone won't work forever, but it'll buy us an extra day or two. They'll figure out that you're staying here and get in touch through me. But then we can meet with them together and it'll be easier."

Patrick nodded. The weight of the situation was already beginning to bear down on him. He was actually glad that he would be at his uncle's house, even if it was freezing. "Okay," he said. "But then what?" Patrick asked.

"Then, we wait. And see what they know or don't know. We'll improvise from there."

LAST OF THE VINTAGE

It was a plan that neither Geoffrey nor his nephew liked, but for different reasons. Geoffrey did not enjoy improvisation. Patrick did not enjoy the cold.

Colour is my day-long
obsession, joy and torment.
~ Claude Monet

CHAPTER NINE

Nick woke the next morning with a staggering headache. "Please tell me I'm not coming down with something," he muttered. Easing himself out of bed he went into the kitchen and made a pot of very strong coffee. While it was finishing he took a hot shower. That seemed to help. He wrapped his thick terrycloth robe around himself tightly and went back to the kitchen.

It was then that he realized that he could not actually smell the coffee. In fact, he could barely breathe through his nose. He was, most assuredly, in the early stages of a cold. The first few sips of coffee confirmed that his throat was raw. "No!" he whimpered. "I do not have time to be sick right now!"

He never got sick when he and Johnson were between cases and had plenty of time. It always happened at the worst possible moment, right when he was busy with something important. He silently cursed the weather for keeping him mostly within the germ-packed indoors, and the stress level that he had imposed upon himself with his stupid assumptions about Dulcie.

His cell phone buzzed on the kitchen counter. He glanced at it. Dulcie. As though she had heard him thinking.

He picked it up and answered. "Hey Dulcie."

"Nick? You sound awful" she said.

"I do? I think I'm coming down with a cold," he answered. The last word came out sounding like 'code.'

"Sounds like you've come down with it already. Are you staying put today?"

"Can't," Nick replied, wincing as he swallowed a large gulp of coffee. "Have to go talk with people. Johnson and I have to start asking questions."

"That's too bad," Dulcie answered. "I just called to see if I could help with anything. And to thank you for the beautiful flowers!"

Nick had nearly forgotten his apology gift. "Glad you like 'em," he said. "I've been kind of a dork lately. Not the gentleman I should be."

"Nick, you're always a gentleman. But sometimes you might jump to the wrong conclusion. Odd behavior for someone in your line of work, I might add."

She was right. Nick had to laugh, although it was actually more of a squawk.

"I'm sorry too, Nick," Dulcie continued. "Having a certain person appear again has just put me on edge. I'll be glad when he's gone. Speaking of that, do you need to keep him here because of the investigation, or can he clear out soon? I'm hoping for the latter."

"Yeah, me too. But at this point he has to stay. I need to talk with everyone that was at the museum the other night. I can probably rule out people who weren't in the boardroom although I'll have to clear that with Johnson too. I'll see what he's been able to find out."

"All right. Let me know if I can help," Dulcie replied.

"I will. Thanks," Nick said. It came out sounding like 'danks.'

Nick poured another coffee as he pressed Johnson's name on the phone. It barely even rang.

"Yeah?" he answered.

"I'm up," Nick said. "Barely. Whaddya got?"

"Man, you sound terrible!" Johnson said, ignoring his partner's question.

"I know. Have to get some aspirin or something. I don't even know what I've got here."

"Hey, don't take anything yet! Last time I got sick I got this stuff that was like a miracle!"

Nick rolled his eyes. "Should I remind you that we're police officers and that swapping prescription medication is kind of illegal?"

"It's over-the-counter stuff," Johnson huffed. "And it worked great for me. Got rid of the headache, opened the sinuses. I was a little light-headed, but still…"

"Okay, okay I'll try it," Nick said. He was feeling worse by the second.

"You can't drive though," Johnson added. "I'll be over in ten minutes." He hung up the phone.

Nick made toast then went back in his room to put on the multiple layers of clothing that had become the wardrobe staple of late. He heard a tap on the door.

Johnson scurried in quickly with a small container of multi-colored capsules.

"How many?" Nick asked.

"Start with two. We'll go from there," Johnson replied. Nick didn't argue. His head had begun to pound again. He gestured toward the coffee pot. Johnson rattled through the cupboard, located a mug, and helped himself. He leaned against the counter. "So once you can actually breathe again, which will take about half an hour I'd estimate, where should we start?"

Nick poured out the rest of the coffee into his cup. "Gotta talk to everyone. Find out who did what, and when. Here's the list," he croaked, sliding his notepad over to his partner.

Johnson leaned over to read it without touching it. He glanced up at his partner who was shaking his head. "Hey, can't be too careful. Don't want both of us sick."

"You're standing in my kitchen drinking coffee that I just made which you poured from a pot that I already touched," Nick reminded him.

Johnson looked alarmed and instantly began washing his hands with a liberal amount of dish soap. He dried them on his pants while looking back at the list. "Half these people we can rule out. I did some digging last night and most of them probably have no idea who Jeremy Plunkett was. They didn't exactly travel in the same circles."

"I can imagine," Nick said. "So who are we down to?"

Johnson glanced at the list again. "To my thinking, it's the wife or the ex-boyfriend, that Spratt guy. She was clearly pretty annoyed with him, and the ex clearly wanted her back. Heck, maybe they were in it together and that show the other night was just that: a show."

Nick thought back. It was a plausible idea. "Anyone else that could be a possibility?" he asked. "What about Spratt's uncle?"

"Yeah, I suppose. Don't know his relationship with his nephew. Or the deceased," Johnson said thoughtfully.

"Then we need to find out," Nick answered. "One last thing. What about Dulcie's ex? Think he might have a reason to want Plunkett gone?" Nick suggested.

"There is the wine connection, but nothing more than that. They'd never met, that I know of. Can't imagine why Brendan MacArthur would have a beef with Jeremy Plunkett."

"Yeah, me neither. But that's a good thing. The sooner we clear him, the sooner he's out of here, and that would make both me and Dulcie very happy."

"Don't let it cloud your judgment though," Johnson reminded his partner. "Especially in your current state."

"Agreed. Good point," Nick replied. "Let's do this: you make the call when you believe we've cleared the Scotsman's name and tell him he can leave. Deal?"

"Deal. Although, I gotta admit, he annoys the crap outta me almost as bad as you," said Johnson.

Nick laughed. His headache was starting to fade. He thought he could actually inhale slightly through his right nostril. "Hey, I think that stuff is working," he said.

"Told ya," Johnson crowed.

"In fact, I just had a brilliant thought. Let's talk to Dulcie's brother and find out what he knows about Brendan MacArthur. Those two seemed to get along pretty well. Dan might even agree to ask Brendan a few questions for us that might get some different answers from what we'd hear."

"Good idea," Johnson said. "Can't think why Dan would like him, but then I don't think Dan dislikes anybody. That kinda guy."

"Yeah. Hey, maybe he's the one who did it. Isn't it the happy-go-lucky type that always ends up being the axe murderer?" Nick mused.

"May I remind you that that's your future brother-in-law you're talking about?" Johnson said with mock sincerity.

"Let's not get ahead of ourselves here," Nick answered. "One day at a time."

"Don't tell me you haven't thought about it," Johnson added.

Nick pointedly took his partner's coffee cup away and put it in the sink. He put on his jacket, shoved the container of pills into the pocket, and headed for the door.

Johnson followed him, grinning.

ॐ

Dulcie arrived at work early that morning ready to test the new security system. After the painting had been removed on the previous afternoon, the installation crew had arrived from Boston and worked into the evening, long after the museum had closed. Dulcie had stayed, feeling that she was obligated to oversee the project. She knew that it wasn't her fault that the painting had gone on display without the required security – after all the exhibit organizers had failed to notify her – but she still felt somewhat responsible for the mix-up.

Cradling a large mug of coffee in her hands after only four hours of sleep, Dulcie watched as one of the workers on a ladder adjusted a nearly invisible sensor high on the wall, while another stood beside Dulcie with a laptop.

"Your motion sensors attached to all of the artworks are great. They'll tell you if a work is being moved and track it in real-time. But they only alert you once something is removed and by then, damage could easily be done. This system detects movement within about three feet of the painting, a range that's outside of arm's length."

Dulcie nodded. "Is it on right now?" she asked.

"Yes. We're trying to get the range right. See Annie adjusting it up there? Each time she does, I can see the range right here," the technician said as he pointed to the screen. Dulcie saw the wall where the painting would hang and a block of transparent red in front of it. "It's red because the sensor is picking up the motion, in this case from the sensor itself." The technician eyed it intently as it inched along in front of the space on the wall. "Okay, good! That's it!" he called up to the woman above them. She climbed down.

"That's fabulous!" Dulcie said. "Does it stay on all the time, or do we turn it on and off?" she asked.

"You can turn it on and off, but we advise that you just leave it on. The sensor up there is connected to the building's power supply. As long as you have power, it has power. Of course it also has a back-up battery."

Dulcie turned to her head of security standing on the other side of the technician. "Think it'll work, Andy?" she asked jokingly. He nodded without smiling. Andrew was not known for his sense of humor.

"Do we need to turn it off when the painting is hung?" Dulcie asked.

"Not unless you want to. It's a silent alarm. I'll go through everything with Andy here so that his team knows the alerts and how to reset it if need be."

"Perfect," Dulcie replied.

Rachel had just clomped through the main door. She shook the snow from her coat over the rug at the entrance. Glancing up, her eyes widened in surprise as she saw Dulcie.

"Wow! Did you stay here all night?" she asked.

"Feels like it," Dulcie said.

"Are we ready?" Rachel asked, now stepping out of her boots. She walked in her stockings over to the front desk, reached behind, and pulled out a pair of stylish pumps that she slipped on without looking down.

"I'll have to remember those are back there," Dulcie said, surprised. "Might have to steal them at some point."

Rachel sighed. Her boss was so well prepared with everything except her own wardrobe. "I've already stashed a pair in your size," she said. "They've been there for a couple of months now," she added.

"If only I'd known!" Dulcie lamented.

"I believe you did," Rachel replied. "You just forgot. Okay, let me hang up this stuff, then we can get to work. Is our little magpie still downstairs?"

Dulcie nodded. *The Magpie*. She wasn't surprised that extra security was required. While most of the works were extremely important, irreplaceable really,

The Magpie was probably the most valuable. Painted by Claude Monet in the winter of 1868-1869 it was an incredible study of snow and light. What made this work so remarkable was that it was one of the first to use colored shadows, something that would become a hallmark of the Impressionists. Monet's bright sunshine cast blue shadows across the freshly fallen snow. A lone magpie was featured perched to one side. It was a painting that Dulcie had always loved.

"Alrighty, then," Rachel continued, emerging from the coatroom. "I'll see if our brilliant preparators are in yet. Let's go get that bird!"

Within an hour they had eased *The Magpie* back to its previous location. Dulcie looked at her watch. The museum was about to open. Perfect timing. "Thanks everyone! You all did a great job!" She turned to go back to her office and caught sight of Nick outside the door. Johnson loomed behind him.

Dulcie walked up to the other side of the glass and said, "Sorry! We're not open yet!"

Johnson pulled out his badge and flipped it open. Dulcie unlocked the door. "Fine! If you put it like that," she laughed. "Come in where it's warm. What can I do for you two today?"

They followed her to her office and once again distributed snowy articles of outwear on the carpet around her desk.

"We've been making a habit of this," Nick acknowledged.

Dulcie looked out the window. The snow was still coming down heavily. "Looks like none of this precipitation is ending anytime soon, either."

"Not helping us at all," Johnson added. "We don't seem to be getting any kind of traction with this case."

"Do you think it's murder?" Dulcie asked.

Nick nodded. "Everything points to that. Maybe not first-degree. Doesn't seem premeditated. But somebody hit the guy for sure, then dragged him to the end of the wharf. Dulcie, could we get a list of people at the opening? And can you let us know which of them went to the wine tasting in the boardroom, too?"

Dulcie opened her laptop and hit a few keys. "Done," she said. The printer beside her whirred into action. She handed the list to Nick.

His eyes widened. "How did you do that?" he asked.

"I had a feeling you guys would need it. I was here last night so I put it together for you. Here's the catch, though. Don't admit to anyone that you got it from me. They'll realize it anyway, but still…. And please, if you could not contact any of them unless you really have to, I would appreciate it. Some of the highest level donors are on that list and I really don't want to annoy anybody."

Nick scanned through the list, leaning over so that Johnson could see it, too. "Anything pop out at you?" Nick asked.

"Other than the folks we've already talked about? Nope. Nobody new here," Johnson said. "But here's a thought. Why don't I go down to that wine bar where the deceased worked and nose around."

"Yeah, that's a great idea except, do you know anything about wine?" Nick asked. He already knew the answer.

"Do I need to?" Johnson looked surprised.

"You might. I have a better idea. Why don't you go talk to Dan and I'll go to the wine bar," Nick suggested.

"Dan?" Dulcie interjected. "Why are you talking to Dan?"

Nick and Johnson exchanged glances.

"Out with it, you two," she said.

"Fine," Nick replied. "We wanted more information on Brendan MacArthur and weren't sure if you'd be objective."

"You don't trust me to be objective?" Dulcie asked.

"Sometimes it's hard to be when you're in the middle of things," Johnson said. "The forest for the trees and all that, you know?"

Dulcie was annoyed but fought to hide it. "I see your point," was all she could manage to say.

Nick attempted to steer the subject away. "What's the name of your friend who owns the wine bar?" he asked.

"Veronica. Tell her I sent you," Dulcie said more curtly than she had intended.

Both men stood and collected their strewn jackets and hats. Nick hesitated. "Thanks Dulcie, I know this has really been a pain for you. You've been such a huge help."

She nodded.

"You know we couldn't do this without you," Johnson chimed in.

Now Dulcie laughed. "All right, stop trying to butter me up! Get out, both of you!"

They clomped to the front door and as they were about to leave, Johnson turned to Dulcie. "Although I might add that none of this would have happened if you hadn't had that wine tasting thing…"

"Out! Now!" Dulcie ordered.

She heard him say something about "…job security for the police force…" as the door closed behind them.

cs

"Now this is interesting! Wait till you hear!" Johnson announced, sliding into the booth seat opposite Nick.

Nick looked up from his notepad. He'd been going through his conversation with the wine bar owner. The cold medicine he'd taken earlier was starting to wear off and his headache had come back.

"Hang on. Lemme get a coffee. You need a refill?" Johnson glanced into Nick's cup. "Nope, you're all set." He left Nick in suspense and chatted with the barista at the counter. Johnson came back with coffee and a sugar-encrusted raspberry scone.

Biting into the scone, he chewed delicately, making Nick wait even longer. He took a sip of coffee, swallowed, then began again. "So, the station just got a call from an insurance company about the case. They passed it on to me and I just had a nice little chat." He paused for effect.

"And?" Nick said. He was used to Johnson's pauses. Nick reached into his pocket and took out the pills that Johnson had given him earlier. Reading the label carefully, Nick then popped off the lid and took out two more, downing them with his coffee.

"Hey, told ya those meds were good, didn't I!" Johnson said, changing the subject.

"They actually are but I'm still hurting, so get on with it. What's interesting?"

You're gonna love this one!" Johnson said, pausing again.

"So…" Nick said impatiently.

"So, our girl Samantha is in line to get a big, fat life insurance payout."

"How big?" Nick asked. He flipped over to a new page on his notepad.

"Half a million."

Nick let out a long, low whistle.

"But there's a catch," Johnson added.

"Isn't there always?" Nick mused.

Johnson nodded. "This one's a doozy. She has to either have children or at least be 'with child' as they said."

"What if she's 'with child' but miscarries?"

"No money. That's part of the catch. She has to actually have the child. And she has to prove who the father is, or was, actually. AND she can't give the child up for adoption."

Nick thought for a moment. His years in law school took over his mind. "If I remember correctly, there are only a couple of stipulations that you can't put on something like that. You can't make someone marry or divorce, and you can't make them change their religion. In court, the child thing would probably hold up."

"So it's valid?" Johnson asked.

"I'm pretty sure it would be. Plus, insurance companies usually do their research well. They know exactly what works in court and what doesn't. They don't like paying out any more money than they have to."

"Hmmmm," Johnson thought aloud, chewing a hefty bite of scone. "So now we need to see if she's preggars."

"Uh, I don't think that's the correct..." Nick interrupted.

"Yeah, yeah. Fine. 'With child' then," Johnson acquiesced. "That's going to be a tricky one," he added.

"That it is," Nick agreed.

"Can't just say to a woman who's husband was killed, 'Oh, I'm so sorry about your loss but by the way, are you pregnant?'" Johnson observed.

"And you sure can't say, "Was your deceased husband the father?" said Nick. "The insurance company must have put a timeline on this. Something like, 'No payout will be made until the baby is born and paternity is determined,' and the mother signs an agreement not to enter the child into an adoption or something like that."

"That'd make sense," Johnson agreed.

"This is getting interesting," Nick admitted. "So we need to find out now if she's pregnant."

"'With child'," Johnson corrected.

"Whatever," Nick said. "We're probably not the right ones to ask that question, but I bet I know who could find out."

Johnson nodded in agreement as Nick pulled out his cell phone and called Dulcie.

Dulcie's phone rang as she stood in the gallery admiring *The Magpie* once again. The museum had a strict No Cell Phone policy, so Dulcie quickly made her way back into her office and shut the door. She pulled out the phone. Nick.

"Hi, Nick!" she answered.

"Hi, Dulcie. Sorry to bother you again," the word came out sounding like 'bodder'.

"You sound awful!" Dulcie exclaimed.

"Yeah. Just took more meds. They were wearing off," he replied.

"You should go home and go to bed! Or maybe you are already?" she asked.

"No such luck," he said.

"No rest for the weary," Dulcie added. "What's up?"

"We have a little bit of a situation here and we might need some help, but only if you're comfortable with it," he began.

"I'll do what I can," Dulcie replied. The line went silent for a moment. "Nick?" Dulcie questioned.

"Yeah, sorry. I was listening to Johnson. Here's what we need. Can you find out of Samantha is pregnant?"

"What?" Dulcie squeaked.

"I know, it seems weird but we need to know. And if Johnson and I barge in and ask her, well, let's just say that's a scene I don't want to have to be part of if I can help it," he admitted.

Dulcie was uncertain of her role in the whole escapade. "Why do you need to know that?" she asked simply.

Nick sighed. His sore throat was getting worse by the second. "Can I explain later?" he croaked. "It hurts to talk."

"Can you put Johnson on?" Dulcie asked. She heard the two men mumbling. Nick spoke again. "He'll call you in a second. He said he isn't going to touch my phone or he'll get the plague, too."

"Sad to say, I think I agree with him," Dulcie confessed. "Okay, promise me you'll go home and rest?" she asked.

"Talk to you later. Thanks Dulcie!" he concluded without promising anything.

Dulcie ended the call. Within seconds her phone rang again. "He isn't going home to rest, is he," she said before Johnson could speak.

He chuckled. "What do you think?" Johnson heard an exasperated sigh from the other end of the line. "Okay, here's the scoop, Dulcie. It seems there was a life insurance policy on Jeremy Plunkett. Samantha gets a very large payout, but only if she has children or is at least *with child*," he pronounced the last words carefully and looked at Nick. He simply sighed in response, which was difficult as he was breathing entirely through his mouth now.

"Wow, that's a doozy!" Dulcie exclaimed. "I assume it's a lot of money?"

"Half a mil," Johnson blurted out.

"Yup, that's a lot. So if she's pregnant, you need to find out if she'd kill her husband to get the money," Dulcie summed up astutely.

"That's the size of it," Johnson said. "Hang on…"

Dulcie could hear Nick's voice in the background.

"Nick says don't mention the money or insurance or anything. Just find out if she's," he paused, "with child."

"I think I can do that," Dulcie acknowledged. "I'll have to think of a reason why I need to talk to her, though. I'll let you know what I find out."

"Perfect. Thanks Dulcie. Nick sends kisses… OW!" The phone went silent.

Dulcie could only imagine the scene taking place between them at that moment. She wondered if Johnson's cell phone was still in one piece.

Dulcie went back out into the gallery. She walked through the new exhibit again. Cold. Snow. Ice. It was everywhere. What would it have been like for Jeremy to be lying in it, his body slowly shutting down? Did he even know? She shivered involuntarily.

That might be the key, though, with Samantha. Not to discuss Jeremy, but to talk about the Little Ice Age. Dulcie could come up with a number of questions to ask about that, and might possibly be able to steer the conversation to other matters as well. It was worth a try, but was it too soon? Would it be too insensitive or presumptuous to assume that Samantha was willing to talk about anything while her husband was still lying in the morgue?

Dulcie tried to put herself in Samantha's place. Would mourning someone preclude everything else? It probably depended on who died, Dulcie realized. In this case, she wasn't certain if Samantha still harbored strong feelings of love toward her husband. Neither of them seemed to be overly affectionate at the opening and wine tasting. To Dulcie, it looked like a relationship gone sour.

She'd have to risk it. What was the worst that could happen, after all? Samantha would be offended and hold Dulcie in contempt for the rest of her life. That was unlikely.

Dulcie went back to her desk and began writing down questions on the Little Ice Age. As always, she wanted to be well prepared.

ख

Geoffrey Spratt liked a good plan. He had stayed up long into the previous night weighing various options and had at last determined a way to move forward. It was the only way, really. He had known that all along. He just had to review any other possibilities thoroughly and rule them out.

The family fortune was intact thanks to him. He had not only managed the money but, more importantly, had managed the family itself to make sure that everything was balanced, that everyone felt they had their fair share. That was the key.

The only wild card was Patrick. He himself seemed oblivious to anything financial. He wasn't a spendthrift, he simply never paid any attention, always assuming that money would be available. The others in the family had noticed and were becoming irritated.

Samantha was the key. Patrick's recent antics were certainly not going to heal any breach in their former relationship. Geoffrey had known, almost since the beginning, that he would have to step in. Radical measures were required.

After the death of her husband, Geoffrey had at first planned to call Samantha and ask her to meet with him. Then he realized that it would put her on the spot. Apprehension would almost certainly make her decline immediately. Her performance at the wine tasting when Patrick had approached her confirmed that.

A note would be much better. A note on the family stationery. A note on the gold-engraved family stationery sent in the matching envelope with the navy-blue lining. It was intended to exude wealth, and it did.

The note was in the guise of a condolence but the subtext was all that mattered. Geoffrey had to assuage Samantha in two ways. First, he needed to flatter her and second, he needed to convey the benefits of the Spratt family wealth while reminding her of her comparative lack of funds.

Both goals could be accomplished with the same topic. Normally, Geoffrey thought, women would be flattered by compliments on their appearance. Not Samantha. Her entire world was her work, and not her 'weather girl' job. It was science. He knew that he needed to praise her skills as a scientist. He needed to hint that her research work should continue. And he needed to connect both of these to Patrick and a renewed relationship with him.

The note, now safely tucked inside the austerely lavish envelope read:

Dear Samantha,

I cannot convey how saddened we are at hearing of your loss. I know that you and Patrick parted ways long ago, but both he and I have wished nothing but the best for you. We were delighted by the success of your career. Patrick has mentioned, many times over during the past few years, how brilliant you always were in the realm of meteorology and how he hoped that you would eventually return to research. He thought your talents were wasted on the daily forecast, although I realize that not only is it a great service to the public at large, it was also the best option for you and your husband as a couple. Sometimes these things are more important.

This loss will take time to heal, but I hope that once you have been able to move forward again you will continue with your chosen career and the work that makes you happy. You certainly deserve that and more.

Please let me or Patrick know if we can help in any way during this difficult time.

Your friend,
Geoffrey Spratt

He had proofread it twice, smiling each time. Yes, it certainly conveyed exactly what it should. He just needed to coach his nephew in how to handle the situation properly, gain Samantha's trust, and win her back. Geoffrey Spratt was not a religious man, but he now looked toward the heavens in silent prayer that Patrick wouldn't screw it up.

ა

The winter sun evidently had been incapable of warming anything during the day, and now cast long shadows as it began to brush the horizon. It wasn't even five o'clock yet, and it was getting dark. Dulcie had lived in Maine for the better part of her lifetime, but still could not get used to the short winter days.

She now sat at the wine bar owned by her friend, Veronica, the very same wine bar where Jeremy had worked. Dulcie had chosen the location purposefully. Veronica would be able to help. Dulcie also thought that since Jeremy had worked there, she would be able to steer the conversation in that direction more readily. Dulcie's primary motive for suggesting this particular meeting place, however, was to see if Samantha would order a non-alcoholic drink. Dulcie had tried to remember if she had seen Samantha drinking champagne at the museum exhibit opening but her memory failed her.

Dulcie and Nick had decided they both would meet with Samantha and had planned carefully. Dulcie would arrive first, well before the appointed time she had set with Samantha, and have a glass of wine in front of her. When Samantha arrived, Dulcie would offer condolences and talk with her for a moment. Meanwhile, Veronica had been instructed to wait until Nick arrived before taking his and Samantha's orders for drinks. Nick, who was of course hiding in the shadow of a nearby doorstep, would wait a bit after he had seen Samantha enter, then would join all of them.

Nick would order only seltzer water, citing his cold and the medicine he was taking. This would give Samantha the option of doing the same and would spark a brief conversation about one's health, alcohol and medication, and, with any luck, pregnancy.

It was a risk having a man present when attempting to spark a conversation about pregnancy, but it was the only way that Dulcie could think of to come close to raising the subject. Besides, she knew that she couldn't talk with Samantha about Jeremy's death on her own without raising some suspicion. Best to have it out in the open that the detectives were looking into it.

Samantha arrived and Dulcie greeted her warmly. As Samantha took off her coat, Dulcie stole a glance at her midsection. Unfortunately, Samantha was wearing a long, bulky sweater that revealed nothing. She hiked herself up on the barstool.

"I think Nick will be along soon," Dulcie began. "Ah, here he is!" she added as he came through the door. He hung up his coat and took a seat on the other side of Dulcie.

Veronica appeared on cue. She had made it a point the day before to visit Samantha to offer her condolences. As Jeremy's former boss, it was expected. Now she smiled at her and said, "Good to see you again. I hope you're doing okay."

Samantha nodded. She was actually feeling better than anyone realized. "I'm holding up," she said.

"I'm glad to see you in here. Jeremy loved this place and we were so grateful that he worked with us. He had such a talent."

Samantha felt as though she was going to scream. It was still all about Jeremy and wine. But she had to hold on for just a little while longer. "He was happy working here," she managed.

Veronica smiled. "What can I get you two?" she asked looking back and forth between Nick and Samantha.

"Just a seltzer water for me," he said. "I'm in the throes of a rotten cold right now and with these meds I've been taking, I'm afraid anything stronger would nock me flat."

Veronica nodded in agreement. "And you?" she asked Samantha.

"I'll have the same," she said simply.

Dulcie felt Nick elbow her.

"Have you been sleeping at all?" Dulcie asked Samantha.

"Not really," she replied.

"Wine, or something like it, might help?" Dulcie suggested.

"No, I really can't drink anything right now," Samantha said flatly.

The subject seemed closed. Dulcie sighed.

When Veronica returned, Nick decided to appear to act in his official capacity and ask questions. He went through the usual routine. Did Jeremy have any enemies? Did anyone appear to behave unusually? Did

Jeremy behave in an odd manner on the day of the event? Was there anything that seemed unusual?

At this last question, Samantha looked thoughtful. "You know, I was distracted at the time, but now that I'm thinking of it, something did seem strange."

"What's that?" Nick asked. He was trying to keep himself from pulling out his notepad. He wanted this conversation to appear more casual. People opened up more when he wasn't writing things down, he'd discovered.

"It was during the wine tasting in the boardroom," Samantha continued. "As Veronica knows, Jeremy loved his wine. He loved talking about it. He'd go on and on sometimes. It wasn't because he wanted to show off, he was just, I guess 'obsessed' is the right word."

"I can second that one," Veronica concurred.

Samantha continued. "When he was in front of everyone and going through the official tasting, he talked about the the vintage, the history, and all of that. But when he actually tasted the wine, he said very little."

Dulcie thought back to the evening. Samantha was right. Jeremy hadn't said much at that point. "Do you think the wine was a bit off and he didn't want to mention it?" she asked. "Maybe he noticed it with his more sensitive palate but thought that probably no one else would?"

Samantha shook her head. "I don't know. I just think it's a little out of character. But then, he was a little nervous about the whole event. He'd talked about what a big deal it was, how those people were very influential and could help his career. Maybe he just got tongue-tied because of that."

Nick finished his seltzer. He was anxious to leave and write everything down. "I have to go meet up with Johnson," he said. "My partner," he clarified for Samantha. "Don't let me rush you two," he added as he slid off the barstool. Dulcie saw him slip a twenty on the bar as he left. He was thoughtful to the last detail.

Samantha was staring into her glass. She waited until she heard the door close. "You know," she said, looking up at Dulcie. "I thought of another reason why Jeremy might have stopped talking."

"Really?" Dulcie asked.

"I didn't want to say anything with *him* here." She nodded toward the door where Nick had just exited. "It's kind of silly. But I was thinking that Jeremy could have suddenly realized, while he was talking, who Patrick actually was. Which is to say, he was my ex-boyfriend. We were very close, unofficially engaged, really." There. She had done it. Planted the seed.

Dulcie knew that something was odd about Samantha's statement but couldn't quite place it. Did Samantha think that Jeremy was jealous of Patrick? Or fearful of him?

Samantha didn't appear to want to offer anything else, so Dulcie decided to change the subject. "I thought of you earlier today for a very different reason," she said. "I was looking at one of our paintings, *The Magpie*, and I realized that the Little Ice

Age may have been partially responsible for the Impressionist movement."

Samantha giggled. She realized that it was the first time that she had laughed in weeks, even before this whole business with Jeremy. "Really? That seems a little crazy!" she exclaimed.

"Well not entirely responsible, but some of the early paintings by Monet and his contemporaries were snow studies. The artists looked at the way light and mist and other weather conditions changed the colors of the snow and the air. They even started painting shadows as colors instead of just shades of gray."

Samantha was silent for a moment. "It makes sense," she said finally. "The light will refract according to what's in the air. And I would think that white is the best background to really see that," she observed, squinting as she pictured it in her mind. She opened her eyes wide again. "Isn't it interesting that the weather, the climate, has so much affect on everything, including history. What I find odd, sad really, is that we know so much more about the science of it now, but it seems as though we pay attention less. Except for having someone," she pointed to herself, "tell us every day how to dress."

'*She loves the science,*' Dulcie thought. '*And not her current job.*' She said aloud, "Spoken like a true scientist."

"I'm hoping to get back to research some day," Samantha said almost wistfully. She glanced at her watch. "I'm sorry Dulcie, but I should go. I'm meeting someone in a few minutes." She pulled out her wallet from her purse.

"No, no. Nick already took care of this!" Dulcie stopped her.

"That was kind of him," Samantha said. "I hope I've helped." As she reached for her coat, her sweater stretched across her stomach. Dulcie thought she noticed a small bulge. Samantha pulled the coat on and, just before buttoning it, put her hand on her stomach for a brief moment. Then she quickly fastened the thick wool around her, said goodbye to Dulcie, and left.

Dulcie continued to sit at the bar, sipping her wine. "You've helped more than you know, Samantha. More than you know," she said quietly.

"Because she touched her belly?" Nick looked a bit incredulous. Dulcie stood in the foyer of the police station between him and Johnson. "Maybe she's just put on weight and is annoyed by it?" he added.

Johnson grinned. "You've got a lot to learn about women," he said. "*I don't envy you*," he added in a clandestine whisper to Dulcie. Nick glared at him.

"Overweight women don't typically touch their stomachs. Or anyplace else where they've put on weight. They don't want to draw attention to it," Dulcie said. "Pregnant women touch their bellies pretty often without even realizing it."

Johnson nodded emphatically in agreement. "Maria did all the time, and so does Cassie now." Their daughter was now grown and about to have a child of her own.

"Huh," Nick acknowledged. "I never knew that."

Johnson looked at Dulcie and just shook his head.

"Well we don't know for sure, but it does point us in that direction," Nick admitted.

"And I'd say that's a motive," Johnson added.

Dulcie glanced outside. It was completely dark and probably even colder than it looked. "I'd better be getting home," she remarked.

"I'll walk with you," Nick offered. They zipped coats, pulled on hats and gloves, waved to Johnson and ventured out into the cold blackness.

"You kind of get used to it," Dulcie said after gasping at the first freezing breath.

"You never get used to it," Nick countered, catching himself as he slipped on an icy patch. "You just convince yourself that you're used to it and that's how we get through every winter."

He heard Dulcie laugh from beneath her scarf. "You're right. We're all really good liars, aren't we. Especially to ourselves," she observed.

They were quiet for a moment, navigating their way along the sidewalk. Dulcie slipped and Nick quickly shot out an arm to catch her. He continued to hold her arm, an unconscious chivalrous gesture.

Dulcie was right. Everyone was a good liar when they needed to be. Some people didn't even realize when they were lying. "Do you think Samantha is lying?" he asked.

"I think she's clearly not telling us everything. I'd love to know more about her and Patrick Spratt, for example. Oh!" Dulcie stopped suddenly and nearly knocked Nick over. "Oops, sorry! I just remembered. After you left the wine bar, Samantha said something about him. Patrick, I mean. She said that she didn't want to mention it with you around."

"Really? What was it?" Nick asked. A gust of wind came shooting down the sidewalk at them. They both stopped and turned their backs to it as it howled by, then returned to their original direction.

Dulcie continued. "Remember that Samantha mentioned how Jeremy had said so little about the wine itself after he tasted it? She thought that Jeremy might have stopped talking so suddenly because he could have realized who Patrick Spratt was. Maybe he had put it all together at that moment, and knew that Patrick was her old boyfriend."

"Does that matter, do you think?" Nick asked. The wind howled down the street again. They both leaned into it this time, still moving forward.

"I'm not sure how," Dulcie nearly shouted as the gust continued. It had picked up bits of ice from the rooftops and now pelted them with it. Dulcie felt it sting on her cheeks. "It could have made Jeremy nervous to have Patrick there," she continued with her head down. "It would be awkward, to say the least."

Nick was reminded of Dulcie's unfortunate encounter with his ex-wife. Awkward didn't even begin to describe it. He hoped she wasn't remembering the same thing. He quickly changed the subject. "Let's go get some dinner. This Italian place is really good I hear," he gestured ahead of them.

Dulcie knew exactly what he had been thinking. That situation, and the subject in general, had been extremely difficult for her. *'Time to let it go now, though,'* she told herself. Everyone had to move on. Especially her. She looked at the stone steps in front of them, then up at the bright red door with a framed menu beside it, and nodded. Yes, she would allow his clumsy attempt to change the subject. Besides, Mia Madre's had the best lasagne in town.

Art is not what you see,
but what you make others see.
~ Edgar Degas

CHAPTER TEN

Samantha read the note over again for the third time. It made her seethe. The audacity of him, to think that she would fall prey to his bait. She knew exactly what Geoffrey Spratt was trying to do. Did he think she was stupid?

Still, this could help. It did show that Patrick was interested in her. And perhaps she could convince that police detective that it was evidence of Patrick wanting her back. Or, at the very least, it was evidence that he could get into an argument with Jeremy over her.

"Patrick thought my talents were wasted with the television job," she said aloud, paraphrasing Geoffrey's writing. It was absurd. Patrick had never bothered to recognize her talents as a scientist. She realized that now. No one else needed to know, however. Yes, this could be excellent evidence that Patrick had a grudge. He could have argued with Jeremy after the party. There could have been a struggle.

Samantha knew that she had to divulge the next piece of information quickly to convince the police that Patrick had killed her husband. She had to tell them that he had been stalking her. Would they believe her?

She remembered what she had screamed at him in the boardroom during the wine tasting. *I've seen you outside my apartment on the street.* That proved Patrick was stalking her, didn't it? She'd said it before everything had happened, before Jeremy....

Yet, there was only one piece of evidence that remained to put Patrick away for good. She had to somehow make sure that either he couldn't account for where he had been after the party, or that someone had witnessed Jeremy and Patrick together. This was getting complicated.

She thought back through that evening. Who might have seen them? Or, more to the point, who might have seen something that she could persuade them to think was Patrick and Jeremy?

Then she remembered Brendan. He had been drinking too much. Who better than a drunk man to convince that he'd seen something he hadn't? Now she just had to craft a way to talk with him.

The mail had come early that day. It was barely noon. "No time like the present," Samantha announced to the empty apartment.

She had thought it would be strange to be there alone, without Jeremy. After the first night, though, she'd realized how often she had been there alone, even when he was alive. He worked late, then often went straight from the wine bar to a friend's house to study long into the night. He would come back in the morning just as she was getting up and sleep for a few hours while Samantha was already at the TV station. By the time she returned home after the six o'clock news, they barely crossed paths again as he headed back to work. On the occasions when they were together, Jeremy was most often closeted in his 'study' as he called it. The somm exam had become his obsession. He had no time for Samantha. Wine was the 'other woman' in his life.

She jarred her thoughts back to her current predicament. "No time like the present," she repeated quietly. She looked up the number for the museum and was put through to Dulcie.

"Samantha!" Dulcie answered with surprise. "It's good to hear from you. How are you doing?"

Samantha realized that she had to begin pretending to mourn. It might look odd if she didn't. She snuffled, then said softly, "I'm holding up all right. I think it just hit me this morning, I was kind of in a state of shock before."

"I understand," Dulcie replied.

"I'm sorry to bother you," Samantha said, "But I have a favor to ask. One of Jeremy's" she choked on the name slightly and swallowed hard, hoping Dulcie could hear it through the phone. "One of Jeremy's friends," she continued, "asked about the wine that the archaeologist has, the one that everyone tried the other night. I think his friend had some idea of buying a bottle although I don't know how he could afford it."

"It would be an investment, from what I've heard," Dulcie stated.

"I want to honor as many of Jeremy's wishes as I can, big or small," Samantha sniffed again. "He would have wanted his friend to find out about the wine. Would you know how I can get in touch with the man who is selling it?"

"Absolutely," Dulcie said. "He's staying at the Regency Hotel. I'm sure you can leave word with them there, and he'll call you as soon as he gets the message."

"Oh thank you, Dulcie. This means a lot to me," she replied.

"Of course. Take care of yourself, all right? And let me know if I can do anything else."

"I will," Samantha answered. "Thanks again."

She put down the phone gently on the coffee table in front of her. Good. On to the next step of her plan.

❦

From those in attendance at the museum event, Brendan MacArthur had managed to come up with six potential candidates who might quietly buy his wine. That wasn't many. He was annoyed with himself for being backed into a corner. It wasn't like him to let things get so out of control.

He jumped at the sound of a polite knock on the door. "Message for you, Mr. MacArthur," a bellhop announced. A paper slid under the door.

Brendan stood quickly, strode to the door and opened it. The bellhop was already halfway down the hall. "Aye! Thank you good man!" Brendan called out. When the bellhop turned around, Brendan held out his hand with a folded bill in it. "For your efforts," he said. The bellhop scooted back, taking it gladly. Brendan knew from experience that one would never regret tipping the underlings. You never knew when you'd need them.

He went back in his room and looked at the message. It was from someone named Samantha Sanders. How did he know that name? Then he snapped his fingers. Right, that incredibly attractive TV reporter. The weather girl. She wanted to meet with him. A friend was interested in the wine.

"This could be pleasant on more than one count," Brendan mused aloud with an almost lewd smile. Whether the smile originated from the prospect of a lucrative sale, or a potential liaison with a very attractive woman was unclear, even to him.

He quickly pulled out his phone and called the number on the note. "Hello, Ms. Sanders! So good to hear from you. This is Brendan MacArthur." He went through the usual platitudes, added his condolences for her recent loss, then got to the point. "I've obviously received your note and would love to talk with you. Have you had lunch yet?" She had not. He suggested a restaurant nearby. She agreed.

Brendan MacArthur happily put down his phone several minutes later, hurriedly changed into what experience had taught him was a more suave outfit, and was out of the room within five minutes.

Samantha was waiting for him when he arrived. He greeted her warmly and sat, taking a menu from the waiter. Brendan ordered a glass of cabernet while Samantha asked for tea.

"Not indulging at this hour?" Brendan asked.

"Not today," she replied. "It's just been so cold out, I feel like tea would warm me up." *'And calm my nerves,'* she thought.

When they had ordered lunch, Samantha began her well-rehearsed speech. "I contacted you because I have a friend who is very interested in your wine," she began. "I meet so many people in the television business, and a couple of them have amazing wine collections," she added.

Brendan's eyes lit up. She would be rubbing shoulders with money certainly, if she didn't already have it herself. "You must know a great deal about wine," he ventured.

She nodded. It was only half true. She had tried to learn early on in Jeremy's pursuits, but lost interest around the same time that he seemed to lose interest in her. "I couldn't help but learn," she smiled softly.

"Jeremy knew so much, and he was an amazing teacher." She swallowed hard for effect.

"This must be so hard for you," Brendan said. "We could do this another time if you like," he added as he thought, *'Keep talking, Samantha. Keep talking.'*

She paused and drank some of her tea. "It's only just hit me what happened. It was all so sudden. And I feel responsible in a way. You see, Jeremy and I argued, and I went home early. If only I had stayed. It sounds so awful that someone hit him, then dragged him over the edge of the wharf. I can't believe there wasn't a witness." She looked up pointedly at Brendan. "When did you leave the museum? Could you have seen anything, do you think?"

Brendan's mind had been focused entirely on wine. Now a thought occurred to him. He was in a great deal of trouble, potentially. He needed to sell the wine and get out of the country quickly. If he helped her, if he had indeed "seen anything" as she asked, it might move things along. It would certainly serve his purpose nicely.

"You know, Samantha, now that you mention it, I do remember hearing an argument. It was pretty late – I don't know what time. I'd had a lot to drink too, I'm afraid. Thinking back though, one of the people did sound like Jeremy. I had just heard his voice earlier that night," he replied.

She was halfway there. He was acknowledging Jeremy. Now she just had to insinuate Patrick into the conversation. "Do you have any idea who the other person could have been?" She opened her eyes widely, innocently, for effect.

He thought for a moment. "I'm not sure. Do you have any ideas?"

They were both playing the same game. Neither knew it.

Samantha shook her head. "The only person that I can think of is an ex-boyfriend of mine. He broke up with me, a few years ago, but in the last couple of months I've suddenly seen him around the city. I've even seen him at night outside my apartment window."

"That's kind of scary," Brendan acknowledged. "Did you report him to the police?"

"No. I really didn't want Jeremy to know. He was so focused on his studies for the somm test. I didn't want to bother him. I thought Patrick would get tired of the whole thing and go away."

Patrick. Could it be Patrick Spratt? He knew the name from the list of potential buyers. The Spratts liked their wine. Suddenly, Brendan remembered Samantha's reaction to someone in the boardroom on the night of the wine tasting. Brendan had not been as drunk as everyone supposed. That person must have been Patrick! She had said something about stalking. Brendan closed his eyes briefly, trying to remember what the man looked like. "Samantha, is Patrick tall and thin, with blond hair?" he asked.

"Yes!" she exclaimed. "Do you remember something?" She was wringing the white cloth napkin in her lap with both hands. She willed herself to stop.

"I think I might. It's becoming more clear. I remember hearing Jeremy's voice outside the museum, and I glanced over toward where it was coming from. I saw what must have been him, along with a tall, thin man with blond hair. He was at the wine tasting too, wasn't he?"

Samantha was nearly shaking. She'd done it! She'd led him into thinking he saw Patrick with Jeremy! "Yes, Patrick was in the boardroom that night. He was there! Do you think…?" She let the sentence fall away.

Brendan had been holding his glass of wine. He now put it down carefully and looked at her intently. "I think we'd better contact the police," he said very severely.

☙

It was already dark when Geoffrey Spratt heard a loud knocking at the front door. He had just poured a pre-dinner Glenmorangie and settled himself in the library. "Who the hell could that be," he sputtered. "Patrick! You expecting someone?" he called to his nephew.

"Nope," Patrick replied from the kitchen. He was mixing himself a drink.

Geoffrey opened the door.

"Sorry to bother you sir, but we're here on important business. Is Patrick Spratt with you?"

Johnson barked. Two uniformed officers were behind him.

"Yes. What's this about?" Geoffrey demanded.

Patrick appeared behind him, drink in hand.

"Are you Patrick Spratt?" Johnson asked. He already knew the answer, but had to make sure it was confirmed.

"Yes," Patrick said hesitantly.

Johnson nodded to one of the officers who stepped forward. "Patrick Spratt, I'm placing you under arrest for the murder of Jeremy Plunkett. I must warn you…" the officer continued.

Patrick dropped his drink on the floor. His face turned gray as the handcuffs were slipped onto his wrists.

Geoffrey began yelling. "What the hell are you doing! My nephew doesn't have the guts to kill a fly let alone another person!" he spat.

The police had located Patrick's coat and threw it over his shoulders. They quickly escorted him outside while Geoffrey continued to yell. "I'll sue all of you!" he hollered.

Johnson remained on the top step. He waited for Geoffrey to stop yelling and breathe. "You can follow us to the station if you like," he suggested. "We do have evidence against your nephew. An eyewitness has come forward."

That was impossible. Geoffrey knew exactly what his nephew had been doing that night, and killing Jeremy Plunkett was certainly not among his activities. Geoffrey had made sure of that.

"They're lying," he stated simply.

It was an odd thing to say at that moment. Johnson sensed this immediately. Usually people said something like, "That's impossible," or "Who was it." The way Geoffrey Spratt had just said 'They're lying' implied that he knew something.

"I would encourage you to follow us to the station," Johnson repeated. He went back down the steps and got into the back seat of the police car with Patrick Spratt.

Geoffrey watched them drive away. He looked back into the house. Patrick's drink was all over the floor. Geoffrey got a towel from the bathroom and wiped up the mess. How had everything spun out of control like this? A blast of freezing air wound its way through the door and Geoffrey realized that he hadn't closed it. He pushed it shut with his foot, then leaned back against it.

What was he going to do now? How could anyone have possibly thought that they had seen Patrick? His nephew was a tall man, but not big or imposing. Nothing about him gave the impression that he could kill anyone. Or even fight someone, for that matter. He was soft. It was a disparaging description, but the only word that fit.

Geoffrey located his keys and his wallet, then pulled on his coat and gloves. He stepped out into the cold, carefully locking the house behind him. He thought of the Glenmorangie longingly. Maybe prison wasn't a bad idea for his nephew after all.

Ↄ

Johnson had returned to Nick's apartment. He'd made his partner stay put during the arrest. Both of them weren't required, and Nick needed to get out of the freezing air and rest.

"So tell me what happened," Nick asked. The medicine had worn off again. His nose was red and the trash can beside him was half full already with tissues. He said 'habbened' rather than 'happened.'

"The usual. Shouting. Denial… the works," Johnson said. He looked tired as he sat down.

"Hey, you're not getting this cold too, are you?" Nick asked.

"Nah. Don't think so," Johnson said. "Healthy as an ox," he added. "I'm just getting frustrated with this one."

"That means you don't think this guy did it," Nick said, honking his nose again into a new white tissue.

"You are correct," his partner admitted.

They were silent for a moment, except for Nick's mild wheezing. "What makes you think that," he asked.

"Cop's intuition. You know," Johnson replied. "When I told him we had an eyewitness, our Uncle Geoffrey said 'he's lying'. First of all, how does Geoffrey know it's a 'he' and secondly, people don't usually say that. They say, 'who was it,' or something like that."

"That is interesting," Nick concurred. "Stick that one in the back of the noggin." He tapped the back of his head, then winced. His headache was worse. Nick started to get up, but Johnson stopped him.

"Whaddya need?" he asked.

Nick didn't argue. "Tea. Coffee. Something hot. And more of this magic pills." He gestured toward the now empty container on the table.

"Okay, I could use a little walk and get out of this germ infested place for a minute. I'll run over to the store. You hang on – I'll be right back." Johnson switched on the electric kettle in the kitchen as he left.

Within ten minutes there was a tap on the door. "It's open, Johnson!" Nick shouted, then winced again.

"It isn't Johnson." Dulcie's voice floated towards him. "And I've brought soup!"

Nick heard her rummaging in the kitchen. "You shouldn't be here," he said halfheartedly. "You'll get sick too!"

Dulcie came around the corner with a tray that held a steaming bowl and a spoon. "I'll take that risk," she grinned.

Nick looked at the soup with some apprehension. Dulcie wasn't known for her culinary skills. He didn't want to be rude, however.

Dulcie couldn't help but notice. "No, I didn't make it!" she said with mock indignation. "It's Hot & Sour soup from the Jade Palace! Now shut up and eat." She plunked it down in front of it.

"Have I told you you're an angel lately?" Nick gurgled as he inhaled the steam from the bowl.

"You can show your appreciation later," she chided.

"You just missed Johnson," Nick said between large spoonfuls. "He'll be back though. Just went to get me meds."

"You have a posse of people doing your bidding," Dulcie commented.

Johnson barged in the door and stopped when he saw Dulcie. "Ah, attending to the sick and needy as well, I see. Aren't we just the altruistic pair tonight?"

Dulcie sniggered.

Johnson handed the bottle of pills to Nick. "That should hold ya for a while," Johnson said

"And this," Nick added, gesturing at the half-empty bowl with his spoon. He quickly put it down and grabbed a handful of tissues as an enormous sneeze erupted from him. Dulcie and Johnson both ducked for cover.

"Sorry, you guys. I'm a mess," Nick said into the tissues.

"No worries. We've all been there," Dulcie said.

Nick pulled himself together and continued eating. Dulcie got up to make herself some tea.

"So Dulcie, to get you up to speed," Johnson said. "Patrick Spratt was just arrested for the murder of Jeremy Plunkett." He and Nick exchanged glances as they heard a crash from the kitchen.

"What?" she said, poking her head around the corner. "I mean, I heard you, but why?"

"Because we've had an eyewitness come forward," Johnson answered.

"Wait a minute. Let me get back in there," Dulcie called out from the kitchen. "Adam, do you want some tea?"

Johnson chuckled. His mother, his wife, and Dulcie were the only ones who called him Adam. "All set, but thanks for the offer."

Dulcie joined them carrying her mug carefully. "Okay, tell me what happened," she said.

"This afternoon I was in the station. Just after lunch. Reception called me out front, and I found Samantha Sanders and Brendan MacArthur standing there."

Dulcie coughed on the last sip of tea she'd just taken. "Wait, who?" she demanded.

"Yup, you heard me right. Seemed pretty odd to me, too. Anyway, I brought them back in to a conference room. They told me that they'd been talking and Brendan had remembered hearing Jeremy's voice outside the museum late on the night of the party, and when he looked over he'd seen someone with him who was tall, thin, and blond. He said it looked just like Patrick Spratt who he'd seen in the boardroom earlier that night."

"He was drunk!" Dulcie exclaimed. "How could he know for sure? That seems pretty flimsy."

"True, but there's more," Johnson continued. "Samantha said that Patrick had been stalking her. He was an ex-boyfriend evidently. And she had a note of condolence from Patrick's uncle that confirmed Patrick had discussed her on a regular basis."

Dulcie blew on the top of her tea. Nick wrestled with the medicine container, trying to open it. "Give me that," Dulcie said. She put down her tea and, with a quick turn of the wrist, pulled off the cap. She handed it back to Nick.

Johnson shook his head in dismay. "You guys are like an old married couple already."

"Shut up," Dulcie and Nick said in unison.

"Adam, that doesn't make sense. I mean, maybe Jeremy and Patrick were arguing, but neither of them seems like the type to get overly heated up. And Patrick *really* doesn't seem like the type to kill someone, especially over an old girlfriend. I don't believe it."

"Yeah, I don't either," Johnson said.

"Me neither," Nick added. His head was tipped back on the chair and his eyes were closed. Dulcie and Johnson looked at each other silently. "I'm not asleep," Nick said. "My eyes just hurt." Dulcie tried not to laugh.

"Hey, I just thought of something," Nick continued without opening his eyes. "What happened to the bottle?"

"What bottle?" Dulcie asked.

"The one that the old wine came out of. Where'd that end up?" Nick replied.

Dulcie thought back. "You know, I'm not sure. I can ask around. Rachel cleaned things up. It was just the glasses so we didn't have the catering staff do it. It would have cost more for the museum."

"Very frugal of you," Johnson chimed in. "Using donors' dollars wisely."

"You have no idea," Dulcie replied ruefully.

"Was the bottle there when everyone left?" Nick asked.

"I'm pretty sure that it was. Wait, I remember Jeremy went over and looked at it. He picked it up and tried to pour out anything that was left, but it was just some sediment," Dulcie said.

"Was he the last one in the room?" Nick asked.

"Aside from Rachel and me, I'm pretty sure that he was," Dulcie replied.

"Interesting," Nick said. "Johnson, did we ever have that piece of glass tested?"

Johnson's eyes lit up. "No, we did not. Just bagged it. But I know where you're going. If it's 19th century glass, we know what hit Jeremy on the head."

"Right. And then we might be one step closer to knowing who," Nick added. He picked up his head and opened his eyes, looking back and forth between the two of them. "See what I can do just from this very chair? I'm like Yoda, I tell you."

"You sound like Yoda," Johnson said. "I think those happy meds have hit you again my friend. I'm clearing out."

"Me too," Dulcie added. She took the dishes and put them in the sink. "You'll be all right here?" she called to Nick from the kitchen.

"Mmmm hmmm," Nick affirmed. His head was against the back of the chair again. "You two just run along."

"Call me when you're awake?" Dulcie asked.

"Of course. You're my angel," he mumbled, his eyes closed again.

Dulcie and Johnson tiptoed out. "What the heck did you give him?" Dulcie asked when they were outside.

"Same stuff as before except this was the nighttime version. He needs to sleep."

"He won't try to drive when he wakes up, will he? He'll still be goofy, for sure." Dulcie worried.

"Not while I have these," Johnson held up Nick's car keys.

Dulcie laughed. "You're awful!"

"I know my partner," Johnson replied simply. "Need a lift home?" he asked. The wind wasn't howling as badly as it had been, but it was still bitterly cold.

"That'd be great," Dulcie said. They scuttled along the icy sidewalk and Johnson opened the car door.

"Oh wait a second here," he said. The clutter in Johnson's car was perpetually monumental. Dulcie had heard Nick talk about it – he always hated riding in Johnson's car – but Dulcie had never actually seen it. It was a mass of shoes, notebooks, various papers, and at the moment an empty donut box. Dulcie slid in, moving the box to the floor.

Johnson eased his large bulk behind the steering wheel. The engine cranked unhappily a few times before turning over. "This weather's been awful on ol' Betty here," he complained.

"I gave up on mine," Dulcie agreed.

Johnson pulled out onto the street. "You know, that was a good question about the bottle," he said.

"I agree. I'm going to call Rachel when I get home. I don't usually bother her after hours, but this seems important."

"Yeah. I think we have the wrong guy locked up," Johnson added.

"Me too," Dulcie said.

Johnson pulled up in front of Dulcie's doorstep. As she unbuckled herself he said, "Hey, can you let Nick know he took the nighttime stuff? I left the daytime one on the kitchen counter. Don't want to be accused of drugging him against his will."

Dulcie nodded, smiling. "If you are accused, though, it's in his best interest, even if he disagrees." She opened the door and hopped out, slamming it shut again quickly. "Thanks, Adam!" she shouted through the closed window and waved.

He waved back, waited to make sure she was safely inside, then rumbled away.

They always say time changes things,
but you actually have to
change them yourself.
~ Andy Warhol

CHAPTER ELEVEN

Geoffrey had slept very little. In fact, he had not even gone to bed. After hearing, several times, the evidence that the police had against Patrick, he had driven home. His glass of scotch had still been sitting in the library. He drank it along with a couple more. When he woke up in the early hours of daylight, he was still sitting in his comfortable leather chair in the library.

The plan was not working. He hadn't accounted for the damned fool getting himself arrested. Geoffrey needed to sort this mess out and quickly.

He reached over for the empty glass beside him and began toying with it, spinning it around on the small tabletop. Maybe most of the plan wasn't working, but one part still would. He had nearly forgotten about it with the other events taking precedence.

Geoffrey stood, groaning softly. He was stiff and sore from sleeping in a chair all night. The room was cold. He checked his watch. Too early to call anyone and get things rolling. Besides, he needed to think a little more and do a bit of research. He lumbered into the kitchen and started a pot of coffee brewing, then went upstairs to take a hot bath.

When he deemed it to be a relatively reasonable hour of the morning, Geoffrey Spratt called the Regency Hotel. He was put through immediately to Brendan MacArthur's room. Geoffrey had taken the liberty of discretely finding out where Brendan was staying as soon as he had learned about the wine tasting. He knew people like Brendan MacArthur. He was one of them. They were never philanthropic without an opportunity for profit.

Brendan answered tentatively. The episode with Samantha and the police had unnerved him, which was not any easy task to accomplish. He wanted the whole situation to be well behind him. He wanted to be gone.

"Geoffrey Spratt," Geoffrey barked by way of a greeting. "Mr. MacArthur, I'll get straight to the point. I understand you have additional bottles of 1869 Château Lafite Rothschild. How many?"

Brendan wasn't prepared for such a direct question. "I beg your pardon, sir?" he replied.

"How many?" Geoffrey repeated bluntly. He liked wasting neither time nor words.

Brendan's mind begin to lurch into gear. Geoffrey Spratt. Patrick Spratt's uncle. Patrick Spratt's *wealthy* uncle. Patrick Spratt's wealthy uncle who had been at the wine tasting. Now things were getting interesting!

Then the realization dawned on him. What if Geoffrey knew that Brendan had been the eyewitness that effectively locked up Patrick? Would the police have told him? Brendan doubted it, but he wasn't completely sure.

"Perhaps we could meet somewhere to discuss this? It would be easier than over the phone," Brendan said. He needed time to think.

Geoffrey was ready. He knew Brendan would stall. It was a classic negotiation tactic, like the used car salesman 'checking with the manager.' He cleared his throat. "I'll meet you in the lobby of your hotel in one hour." He hung up the phone.

Brendan sat back, staring at the phone for a moment. His heart was pounding. Now what? He had to think. He began pacing the room. He wasn't happy with this newly formed habit. It meant he wasn't in control.

This whole situation had become very sticky, very fast. He needed to leave. He needed to get out of the country. First he needed money, however, and this was the source. Geoffrey Spratt. The difficulty would be the price.

Brendan had nine bottles remaining. The vintage had previously sold at auction for over $200,000 each.

He knew he couldn't get that amount if he wanted to move quickly but he needed as much as possible.

An hour later, Brendan MacArthur sat in a quiet corner of the hotel lobby in an uncomfortable armchair. He saw Geoffrey Spratt come in and look around the room squinting. He spotted Brendan and came over. Brendan rose, shook his hand, then sat again.

Geoffrey sat opposite him, hunched forward. "How many bottles do you have?" he said, continuing exactly from where they had left off on the phone.

"How many do you need?" Brendan countered.

"Don't get cagey with me. We both know how this goes. You sell, I buy, no one is the wiser."

"Are you adding to your collection?" Brendan side-stepped the statement.

"I'm investing," Geoffrey replied. "Don't be an idiot."

Brendan had to laugh. Few people were as straightforward as Geoffrey Spratt. It was actually refreshing. "I have nine bottles," he said.

"I'll give you half a million for them all," Geoffrey responded quickly.

Brendan smiled and sat back. "That's quite low. They've gone at auction for…"

"I know what they've gone for at auction. This isn't an auction. You need to sell and keep it quiet. I want to buy. I don't need to buy, mind you. I can certainly find investments elsewhere," he began to stand.

"No, no! I was simply saying that their value is quite high. I'm sure we can come to an agreement," Brendan implored.

Geoffrey sat back down but said nothing.

Brendan thought for a moment. "All right," he said at last. "But I do have one condition for such a low price. I would like the money wired to my account in the Cayman Islands by five o'clock tomorrow. As soon as I see the funds, I'll be at your doorstep with the wine."

Geoffrey wasn't sure about this deal. Brendan had accepted far too quickly. Perhaps Geoffrey wasn't actually going to get the wine and Brendan was just planning to skip town with the money? No, there had been a very public show of this Château Lafite Rothschild and Brendan had said he wanted to auction it off. Geoffrey knew people like Brendan MacArthur. They liked to maintain their connections with those who had money for when there were more things to sell. And the Brendan MacArthurs of the world always had more to sell.

For whatever reason, Brendan needed money quickly which was why he was accepting this ridiculously low offer. Geoffrey left it at that. He stuck out his hand and shook Brendan's. "You have yourself a deal. Get me the account information and I'll wire the funds. I'll expect nine bottles on my doorstep by five o'clock sharp tomorrow."

Geoffrey went back out into the icy afternoon with a much warmer feeling inside. He'd just made an excellent investment.

Brendan sat back in the chair and looked broodingly across the room. Half a million dollars. It wasn't even close to what he'd wanted. In a better situation he could have easily pulled in 1.5 million. But he had to take it. What else could he do?

He should pack. Assuming this transaction went through, and there was no reason why it wouldn't, he would be checking out of the hotel in the morning. He needed to make arrangements. His crew had to be paid, just enough to keep them happy. As always, they didn't need to know how much he was making.

He thought about the murder investigation. Standing in the police station, giving his statement, signing it… he had wanted to bolt and run. The whole thing made him uneasy, and it was not a feeling with which he was overly familiar. But now it was nearly over. Just one more day.

☙

Adam Johnson sat in the cabin of Dan Chambers yacht wondering how it was possible to live in such a small space. By boat standards the room was actually quite large, but Johnson couldn't think of even one apartment he'd lived in during his single days that wasn't at least twice the size. Plus, this particular home bobbed up and down gently as the tide came in. Most would have found it soothing. It was making Johnson increasingly ill.

Dan sat opposite him, legs stretched out in front of him. He was recounting his recent trip to Miami, telling Johnson about the yachts he had coveted the most. When he paused for breath, Johnson finally interrupted him. "Sounds great, Dan. Excellent to get away and not freeze your arse off like the rest of us poor slobs up here," he said.

Dan grinned. "Want a beer?" he asked.

Johnson was on duty, but thought it might settle his stomach. "Got anything light?" he asked.

"Never thought I'd hear those words from you!" Dan joked. "But you are watching your weight these days, I've heard, and I must say it shows!" He handed Johnson a bottle.

Johnson twisted off the cap, took a deep swig, then slowly exhaled. He looked over at Dan. "So we have ourselves a bit of a situation here," he said.

"What's my sister done now?" Dan laughed.

"Nope, not her. But this murder, and we do know that it's murder at this point, kind of has us baffled."

"How so?" Dan asked.

"We've had an eyewitness come forward who says a struggle took place," Johnson stopped Dan as he was about to speak. "Nope, can't tell you who the eyewitness was. But I can say that it seems odd nothing was said until now. It also seems odd who's saying it."

"That does sound like a pickle," Dan replied. "But I don't see how I can help."

"We're hoping that you might have seen something. Anything. Or heard something that night. It's pretty dark here, I know, but you're right on the dock here where the guy was killed. You're kind of our only hope at this point."

Dan took a long drink, then sat back. He closed his eyes for a moment. "Let me think. I'd just come back from Miami that morning. I went to the party at the museum. Trailed our friend MacArthur at Dulcie's request. He was getting a bit loaded and she wasn't sure what he'd say or do. To tell you the truth, I was kind of surprised he'd get drunk at something that was pretty important to him. But then again, he's Brendan MacArthur. He never plays by the rules. Part of his charm." Dan smirked.

"Do you remember when he left? Was it before you?" Johnson asked.

"I didn't really notice. We got through the tricky part of the evening, then we had that little scene with the weather girl screeching at that guy. Hey…!" Dan looked up at Johnson. "That's the guy you have locked up right now, right?"

"Yes, it is. We're trying to keep it quiet."

"Yeah, good luck with that. The gossip mill in Portland is faster than a greased pig," he grinned. "Was that the right metaphor? You get my meaning. Anyway," he said, standing. "I can't be of much help I'm afraid, but I know who, or should I say 'what,' can."

"Yeah?" Johnson said hopefully.

"Yup. Hang on." Dan went up on the bridge and Johnson heard him rummaging through something. He came back down with a laptop. "Here's the thing. While I was away, I set up a camera on the boat. I just wanted to keep an eye on things. I forgot to shut it off until the day after Dulcie's party." He tapped a few keys. A black and white image of the Dan's boat appeared.

Johnson groaned. For a brief moment he'd been excited thinking that this could be the break they needed. A camera that recorded exactly who pulled Jeremy Plunkett's body down the dock. Unfortunately, the camera was set up on the bow and faced down the length of the yacht. Very little of the wharf beside it could be seen. "Thanks Dan, but I don't think this'll help us any," Johnson said.

"Yeah, I see what you mean," Dan added. "Bummer." He toyed with the controls of the video playback anyway, moving the playback time to that evening. "Worth a look maybe. I'll speed this up so we won't be sitting here all afternoon," he said.

Johnson breathed a sigh of relief. Claustrophobia was beginning to set in at this point. They watched the empty boat bob up and down, slowly rising beside the wharf as the tide came in. The clock ticked through the minutes. It reached eleven o'clock. Nothing happened.

Suddenly, the camera jumped. Nothing else changed, but it was as though the boat had been nudged. A moment later it happened again.

What followed next made both men lean forward and stare at the screen intently. A large shadow moved across the boat. "What the hell was that?" Johnson exclaimed.

Dan backed up the video and they watched again, this time in slow motion. It looked very much like a person dragging something down the dock. They replayed it several times.

"Is this just wishful thinking, or are we actually seeing…," Dan didn't finish the sentence.

"Can I take this?" Johnson said, pointing to the laptop.

"Wait, let me just copy the video for you. Hang on." Within moments he had the video on a tiny drive that he handed to Johnson.

"I'll get one of the kids to bring this up for me," Johnson said.

"You're not tech savvy, I take it?" Dan smiled. "Let me do this, too. I'll email it to you and Nick. What's your address?" he asked.

Johnson just stared at him. "Um, wait. I think I know. Uh, dammit. Hold on." He pulled out his phone and dialed.

"Yeah?" Nick answered after the first ring.

"Hey, you sound better!" Johnson replied.

"Feel better. That's what twelve solid hours of sleep can do, evidently. Those were some good drugs you gave me!"

"Spoken like one true cop to another," Johnson quipped. "Hey, I've got Dan here. Can I put him on?"

"Yeah sure," Nick said.

Johnson handed the phone to Dan.

"Hey dude. Glad you're feeling better. We're trying to get a video to you but your partner is having trouble on the tech side," Dan said.

"Doesn't surprise me," Nick replied.

"I'll just email it to you. What's your address?"

Nick gave it to him, then Dan handed back the phone to Johnson.

"What's this about?" Nick asked his partner.

"Tell you when I get to the station. Where are you?" he asked.

"At the station," Nick said.

"Okay, stay put and look at that video. Tell me what you think it is." He hung up. "Dan, you may have helped us immensely or you may have given us total crap," he said, standing up in a slightly hunched posture. He was always afraid he would hit his head on boats.

"Story of my life," Dan mused. "Glad I could help, maybe."

Johnson grunted, shook his hand, and climbed onto the dock carefully.

Nick was scowling at the computer screen when Johnson arrived back at the station. "Thoughts?" he asked.

"Pretty much what you're thinking, I'd say," Nick said. "At the very least we have the time established.

That's more progress than we've made since we started, I think."

"Yeah. I was also wondering if there's any way the forensic crew can look at this and figure out how tall the guy is dragging the body? Triangulate the shadows and such?"

Nick nodded. "Good idea. I'll send it to them. They love stuff like this," he chuckled. "Meanwhile, let's go through the file and see exactly when everybody said that they left the party."

Johnson nodded. "You know, I was thinking. Whoever did this took a hell of a risk dragging the body down to the end of the wharf like that. Anybody could have come by and seen them."

"It's pretty dark. Only that one light that's giving us our shadow. But still…," Nick agreed.

"Must have been someone pretty stupid or pretty desperate," Johnson said. "Okay, lets go back through statements. We may have to call in some folks again. Nobody'll be happy about that," he added.

Nick had already pulled up the files on his computer. He kept the video running in a continuous loop in the corner of the screen.

ଔ

Samantha ran to the bathroom and heaved into the toilet for the second time in an hour. The waves of nausea had been horrific. It was a futile exercise –

there was nothing left in her stomach – but for some reason her body didn't seem to know that. She sat down on the cold tile floor, leaning against the door of the towel closet.

When she felt almost normal again she staggered to her feet, opened her computer, and typed in 'morning sickness.' "Although it's afternoon, ironically," she said aloud. She scrolled through the gibberish about why it happens then found information on 'relief from.'

Peppermint or ginger. Either was supposed to help. She decided to try the peppermint. She'd had peppermint tea a while back. Maybe it was still in the cupboard?

She turned on the kettle then looked through the cupboard. Thankfully, it was still there. As she put it on the counter and reached for a mug, she heard a knock at the door. She froze.

Samantha tiptoed over to the door and looked through the peephole. The two detectives stood outside. She took a deep breath and opened the door.

"Sorry to bother you. We tried to contact you on the phone but didn't get an answer," Nick said. "Could we ask just a couple of quick questions?"

Samantha managed to say, "Yes, give me a moment," before hurtling through the door of the bathroom again. Thankfully the distress was brief this time. And quiet. She splashed cold water on her face, then returned to her guests.

"Sorry about that," she said as nonchalantly as possible. "What can I help you with?"

Johnson eyed her intently. Nick said, "Quick question. Do you remember what time you left the party the other night?"

The kettle reached a boil. Samantha went into the kitchen, thankful to have a moment to think. "Would you like some tea?" she called out.

"No, thanks," the two men said in unison.

Samantha came through to the living room cradling the mug in her hands. "Have a seat," she gestured. The two men sat uneasily. "Jeremy called me a cab. It was right after the wine tasting. I was glad to get out of there. I just can't believe that Patrick could have... well...," She looked down into the steam from her tea. "If only I had stayed, it would have been different," she concluded with wide eyes.

"I know this has been hard," Nick said. He couldn't count the number of times he had said that exact sentence over the past few years. He hoped that it still sounded sincere.

"Did you stay home for the rest of the night?" Nick asked.

Samantha looked at him with surprise. "Yes, of course I did! Where would I have gone?" If it was possible, her eyes were now even wider.

"It's just routine to ask," Nick reassured her. "How have you been holding up?" he inquired.

"Not terribly well," she said. "And now I'm under the weather it seems. My mother is coming tomorrow to stay for a few days. We have to arrange the funer...," she choked back a sob on the last word and quickly swallowed a large mouthful of tea.

"I understand," Nick said. "Well, we won't take up any more of your time," he added. "We can see ourselves out."

Samantha simply nodded as they quietly left.

Neither of them spoke until the reached the street again. It was getting dark but fortunately the air was still. Their breath floated around them in large clouds. "You were quiet," Nick observed.

"I was looking around," Johnson said. "Did you notice anything different?"

"Not really," Nick said. "You did?"

"Ummm hmmm. When we were there before, the day we broke the news, there was a wine rack with glasses on it. It was in the living room behind the chair where she was sitting. It's gone now."

"Huh. That's interesting. Maybe she gave it to a friend? A remembrance kind of thing?" Nick guessed.

"Yeah, maybe. But here's another thing. She's preggars for sure," Johnson stated.

Nick turned and gave his partner an incredulous look.

"She is, I tell you," Johnson maintained. "She had that little episode when we first got there. Then she was drinking peppermint tea," he paused.

"Yeah, it smelled good," Nick said. He stopped. "Hey, I can breathe through my nose again!"

Johnson shook his head and kept walking. Nick hustled and caught up with him. "And also," Johnson added, "She has that rounder look to her face."

"What?" Nick said. "What are you talking about?"

"Look, you ask Dulcie," Johnson told him.

"Who has most decidedly not, to my knowledge, ever been 'preggars' as you say."

"You sure about that?" Johnson goaded his partner.

Nick glared at him.

"Look, I'm just saying that when Maria was pregnant, that pretty much described her for a while. Suddenly sick as a dog, always had peppermint something, and her face looked rounder even before her belly did. Oh, and like Dulcie said before, Maria would always put her hand on her belly."

"So what you're saying is that Samantha could have taken a cab home, then gone back to the museum, waited for her husband, whacked him on the head, then dragged him off the wharf."

"Yup," Johnson replied.

"You're right. It's entirely possible."

"And, I think that marriage wasn't as rosy as she'd have folks believe," Johnson added.

"Plus, half a million dollars is pretty good incentive," Nick replied.

"And she is conveniently preggar...I mean pregnant. With child." Johnson concluded.

They were both silent.

"So who else have we got?" Nick asked. He stuffed his hands deeper into this pockets. They were already numb from the cold. "Patrick, the ex-boyfriend who someone pointed the finger at. What about Patrick's uncle? That note he wrote to Samantha seemed like both the uncle and Patrick wanted them to get back together."

"True," Johnson said. "What did Geoffrey Spratt say about what he was doing that night?"

"He says that he and Patrick left around ten-thirty."

"To his mansion on the West End," Johnson added.

"Correct," Nick replied.

"So he could have pretty easily come back down to Commercial Street, parked, and waited for our poor friend to come out of the museum."

"Then smack him on the head and drag him over the edge," Nick finished. "Something just doesn't add up though. It doesn't feel right. If it's a crime of passion, where's the passion? Nobody seems to have had that much of it in them. But at the same time, it doesn't really feel calculated, either. Clearly it was opportunistic." He groaned in annoyance, but then had another thought. "Hey, what'd we find out about that bottle?" he asked Johnson.

"I heard back from the lab and the piece of glass is old, for sure. Dulcie hasn't said if they found it when they cleaned up the room, right?" Johnson replied.

Both men looked at each other, then turned in unison down the next street toward the museum. Johnson pulled his coat sleeve up with a gloved hand and looked at his watch. "Ten to six. Think she's heading home now?" he asked.

Nick laughed ruefully. "Nope. She's still there. Hope she's not in a meeting or something though."

They reached the museum and tromped into the foyer. Rachel was just walking through. "Ah, gentlemen! You always bring us happiness and good cheer!"

They both snickered. "Can we just go straight in?" Nick asked.

"Be my guest," Rachel gestured.

"That's what we call 'sass'," Johnson lisped.

Dulcie looked up as they came through the open door of her office. "Ah! To what do I owe the pleasure? And Nick, glad to see you, um, non-comatose!"

Johnson slapped him on the back, making him cough. "Modern medicine, my friends! Modern medicine!" he announced.

They both sat, loosening their coats. "We were just going by and wondered if you'd found out anything about the bottle?"

"Yes, the Lafite bottle," Dulcie replied. "I talked to Rachel. She remembers seeing it as people were leaving, but does not remember it being there when she was cleaning up."

"Does that mean it might have been there but she doesn't recall, or that it wasn't there because she would have remembered?" Nick asked.

Dulcie's eyes lit up. "Astute question! The latter. Rachel is also very astute."

"Thank you!" They heard a voice call out from the hallway.

Johnson got up and shut the door. He sat back down. "Here's why that's interesting. The piece of glass in Jeremy's collar was clearly from an old bottle. The lab told me that older ones often still had bubbles in the glass. He couldn't tell me how old, but definitely not one of our modern, machine-made ones."

"So we're now concluding that Jeremy was hit with the empty bottle of Château Lafite Rothschild?" Dulcie asked.

"Looks like it," Johnson said.

"That just seems strange," Dulcie said, leaning forward on her desk. "Why would someone take that bottle, and why would they hit him over the head with it?"

"Maybe it was what they had on hand at the time?" Nick said.

"No, they would have had to go back up there after everyone had left. That's not opportunistic. But why?" Dulcie asked.

Both men shook their heads.

"We do have one lead thanks to your brother though. We've got a shadow of someone dragging something down the dock. It happened at four minutes after eleven that night," said Johnson.

"That's actually right after I remember seeing Jeremy leaving. He was one of the last to go. I think he liked mingling with the well-to-do wine aficionados." Dulcie added.

"Don't we all," Johnson quipped. "Oh, and I'm with you on the weather girl being pregnant thing."

"Forecaster," Nick and Dulcie chorused.

"Huh?" said Johnson.

"Never mind," Dulcie interjected. "Did you find out for sure?"

"No but she was briefly sick in the bathroom, then had peppermint tea, and her face looks rounder," Johnson said.

"I'd say you nailed it, Adam," Dulcie agreed.

Nick looked from one to the other. He took a deep breath. "Why do I feel like we're going in circles?"

"Because we are and we're missing something," Dulcie replied.

There was a tap on the door. Rachel poked her head in. "Are you guys going to have your clandestine meeting for much longer? Security is going to lock up. You'll have to let these gentlemen out with your key," she said to Dulcie.

"Nope, that's fine. We were just leaving," Johnson said. He glanced back at Nick. "Er, I mean, I was leaving anyway."

"You're right. Me too. I have to catch up doing what I should have done when I was sleeping in this morning," Nick said.

"You do look better!" Dulcie complimented.

"I feel so much better. Johnson's magic pills. I should still get more rest though. Don't want it coming back," Nick replied.

"Right. Good idea," Dulcie said. "I'll see you two later then."

They nodded as they pulled their coats up high around their necks and bustled out. Dulcie heard the security guard locking the door behind them. His footsteps echoed across the marble floor as he went back downstairs to his office lined with video screens showing the entire museum. Dulcie stood and leaned out around her doorframe. Rachel had gone home as well.

It was only six o'clock but the sky was already black. Winter nights were long in Maine. Long and cold. Dulcie walked through the quiet, cavernous main hall and went in to the Little Ice Age exhibit.

The lights had been dimmed. The paintings, mostly white, wintery scenes, seemed to eerily glow. Dulcie loved being alone in a museum. It seemed as though the artists were there with her, talking to her.

Snow, ice, cold. People trying to make the best of things when year after year they had meager food, cramped living quarters, perhaps too little firewood. And yet some of the greatest works in history were created because of this. Mary Shelley's *Frankenstein* was the result of a competition among Shelley and her friends when they were stuck indoors during the infamous 'Year Without a Summer.' Antonio Stradivari's violins were thought to produce such beautiful sound because their wood was the result of the slow growth of trees during the overly cold years. Monet's *The Magpie* was yet another example, an exploration of light and color that took place because of the snow. She stopped in front of it, marveling once again at the hues.

Dulcie heard a rapping at the museum's front door. At first she thought it was the wind rattling it, but then she heard it again. She walked back into the main hall and saw Brendan MacArthur standing on the other side. Dulcie gestured for him to wait, then hurried in to her office to get her key. She came back with it, twisted it in the lock, and pushed open the heavy glass.

'*What could he want?*' Dulcie thought. She was a bit uncomfortable being alone with him, but he looked sober enough, she decided. Besides, there were security cameras everywhere.

"My lass, Dulcie!" His voice boomed through the empty room. He kissed her on the cheek.

"To what do I owe the pleasure?" Dulcie asked, dodging a kiss on the other side.

"I've just come to say goodbye," he said.

Dulcie looked surprised. "Really? Is your work done?" she asked.

"Aye, for the most part. Nothing more can be done on the wreck until springtime, and I'll leave it with an enthusiastic graduate student or adjunct professor trying to make a name for himself," he explained.

'*Or herself,*' Dulcie thought. "That's generous of you," she said instead.

"I am generosity itself," he boasted.

"Ah, yes," Dulcie replied, trying to keep all hints of sarcasm from her voice. She decided to change the subject.

"Did you get a chance to see the exhibit?" she asked.

He craned his neck to see behind her. "Actually, I did not! And I don't mind saying that, knowing your impressive skills, I'm sure it's perfection. Shall we take a turn through?"

'*What is this about?*' Dulcie thought. "Of course," she said, hoping that she was masking her thoughts. "I just need to lock the door first so no one comes wandering in." She gestured toward the gallery. "I'll be right behind you," she added.

Dulcie locked the heavy glass door, then joined Brendan in the gallery. He was standing in front of Raeburn's *The Skating Minister*. "Brendan, I am sorry that the other night didn't work out as planned," she mentioned as she walked up beside him.

"The other night?" he asked.

"The wine tasting?" she prompted.

"Oh that! Actually that worked out quite well," he replied.

Dulcie was astonished at his callousness. Perhaps he didn't remember everything? "Well, a man did die," she chided.

"True, poor soul, but that was later. We were done by then," he replied. He turned to Dulcie quickly. "Actually, I wanted to mention something about that," he said. "I have to confess. I was the witness who saw a tussle between that poor man and the other one who must have killed him. Patrick Spratt. I've given my statement to the police. They haven't asked me to stay, but I'd rather not contact them to get permission. I'm going through some, uh, delicate negotiations at the moment, you might say. Since your current lover happens to be the detective on the case, I thought I could rely on you to smooth things over in case they ask about me. I mean, they really shouldn't have need to talk with me again. Just tell them that I'm on a dive site in Micronesia, all right? There's a good girl."

Dulcie didn't appreciate the direct reference to Nick as her 'current lover,' and she bristled at being called a 'good girl.' She also didn't understand why she would need to lie for him, because they both knew that was exactly what he was asking.

She turned and walked away from him for a moment. None of this was making sense. His sudden appearance in Maine. The risk he took wreck diving in the icy Atlantic in January. The wine. A murder.

She now stood in front of *The Magpie*. She glanced over at the identification card on the wall. Monet. 1869. France…

Château Lafite Rothschild.

Suddenly, it all fit. The answer flooded over her, leaving her shaking. She looked over at Brendan, then her eyes darted behind him toward the gallery entrance.

She had just given herself away. He took one step toward her. She backed up.

"So you've worked it out," he said quietly. "I shouldn't be surprised. You've always had the quickest wit of any woman I've known," he chuckled, emphasizing the word 'woman'. "You see, the problem arose when you invited that damned somm to be a part of everything. I knew that he would suspect right away. My bloody luck that you had a Master Sommelier candidate in this little backwater village."

"I'm not sure what you're talking about, Brendan. Jeremy said that the wine was excellent," Dulcie's voice was shaking. She tried to convince him that she didn't understand, to make him still believe that he had gotten away with it.

He shook his head and took another step toward her. "Don't play the fool with me, Dulcie. We both know exactly what happened. It was what Jeremy *didn't* say. Yes, it was an excellent Lafite. However, as Jeremy so astutely realized, it wasn't an *1869* Lafite. It was considerably more modern. I'd tasted the 1869 that I'd dredged from the deep, and it was complete trash. I knew Jeremy had his suspicions. But it was when he went back for the bottle that I knew I had a problem. You see, I saw him sneak back upstairs. I knew what he was after. He was going to take the bottle and get it tested. Then he'd prove me to be a fraud. And probably boost his own credibility as a discerning somm, the little bastard," Brendan concluded with disgust.

Dulcie swallowed hard. The room had begun to swim around her. Brendan was still talking.

"When Jeremy left, he was wearing a bulky coat and I knew exactly what was underneath it. I followed him and confronted him outdoors. He reached for the bottle immediately of course to protect it. I grabbed his arm to wrestle it away. I'm a lot bigger than him, so both he and the bottle fell. He hit his head hard and was knocked out.

"I only had one option then. Get him out of sight. I dragged him to the end of the dock and pushed him onto the ice. On the way back I grabbed the damned bottle so I could get rid of it."

Dulcie felt sick. Her knees could barely hold her. But she had to buy time so that she could think of a way to escape. "Didn't you see that it was broken?" she asked.

"What was broken?" he looked surprised for a moment. "Oh yes, the bottle!" He eyed her intently. "How did you know that?"

"A piece of glass was found in Jeremy's collar," Dulcie replied.

Brendan rolled his eyes as though it was all one big joke. He was walking toward her again. "It all could have worked so well. Samantha came to me *suggesting* that ridiculous story to point the blame at Patrick. Of course I was only too willing to be an eyewitness," he crowed. "It was the perfect way to end this thing. And to top it all off, in a twist of irony, Patrick's good uncle is buying the rest of the bottles! I'll have the money by tomorrow!" Brendan's eyes gleamed.

"All you had to do, my sweet little Dulcie was play your part. But no, you've never been able to do that from the start, have you?"

"What do you think you're going to do now?" Dulcie said. "We do have a security camera watching every move you're making," she said.

Brendan snickered. "Did I ever tell you how good I was with a slingshot as a child? I used to practice in school knocking pencils out of my classmates' hands. A rubber band and a penny was all it took. It was so much fun!"

Dulcie glanced up at the camera in the corner. It was pointed toward the ceiling.

"Terrible accidents happen all the time, you know. This marble floor can be so slippery. And it's quite hard as well."

He lunged toward her. Dulcie sidestepped out of the way as quickly as she could. She was facing *The Magpie*, about thirty feet away and remembered the new security system that the museum had just installed. She hoped that it would work. She'd never been a good shot. She hurled the keys that she was holding at the painting. Then she screamed as she felt herself falling to the floor.

The world was a blur but she heard Brendan swearing. Footsteps running on the marble. Someone pounding on the glass door of the foyer. More footsteps....

Dulcie woke up surrounded by people. Paramedics were checking her head. Someone held ice to it and she winced. Her focus began to clear and she saw Nick's face hovering above her.

"Brendan did it," she said simply.

"Exactly what I thought," Nick said. "The bastard nearly killed you! He said you slipped but I don't believe it."

"Yes. No! I mean," Dulcie couldn't get the words out right.

"Shhh, don't talk," one of the paramedics said.

Dulcie looked pointedly at Nick. "Brendan killed Jeremy," she clarified in as loud a whisper as she could muster.

Nick's eyes were wide. "You're sure?"

"He told me," she whispered again.

Nick glanced over at the person taking Dulcie's pulse. "Is she going to be okay?" he asked.

"She'll have a hell of a headache, but she should be fine. We'll have to take her to the hospital just to check her out though. Make sure it isn't concussion," he said.

Nick looked back at Dulcie. "I've gotta find Johnson. I have to go. I'll see you in the hospital as quickly as I can," he said.

"Go," she replied simply and attempted a smile.

He squeezed her hand and she saw him leave the gallery.

Nick worked quickly. Brendan had managed to slip away from the museum. Nick had a feeling he knew where to find him. He'd already looked up the fishing boat that Brendan had rented for his dive excursion. Nick contacted Johnson, then immediately called for backup as well.

The boat was near the old dry dock at the far end of Commercial Street. Nick ran down the street, hoping he'd get there in time. He saw cruisers coming down the street in the opposite direction. They stopped and police flooded out, along with Johnson. Nick sprinted toward them. "Wait! He could start firing on us if we all go down the dock!" Johnson yelled. They heard a shot. "COVER!" Johnson bellowed, and each of them immediately ducked behind the nearest object.

Nick scuttled over to where Johnson was crouched behind an empty oil drum. "Don't think we'll have to worry a whole lot," Nick said.

"Huh?" Johnson panted.

"Look," Nick replied.

Marine patrol vessels were closing in on the little fishing boat that had just pushed off from the wharf. It was no match for them. Their spotlights cast a blinding glow off the black water. Nick and Johnson watched as patrol officers boarded the fishing boat and, a few moments later, hauled a handcuffed Brendan MacArthur over the side into one of the sleek blue vessels.

The object of art is not
to reproduce reality,
but to create a reality
of the same intensity.
~ Alberto Giacometti

CHAPTER TWELVE

The conference room in the police station was stuffy. Nick cracked the window slightly. Cold air whistled in. "Let me know if this is too much for anybody," he said over his shoulder.

Samantha breathed a sigh of relief. She was feeling overheated, nauseous, and otherwise miserable. It had nothing to do with her pregnancy and everything to do with the pair that sat opposite her: Geoffrey and Patrick Spratt. She reached into her purse for the tin of peppermint Altoids.

Dulcie sat beside her trying not to squirm. The entire situation was uncomfortable, but she felt at least partially responsible for the series of events and had insisted that she should be there.

Johnson blustered in and hefted himself into the chair at the far end of the table. Dulcie noticed what appeared to be pastry crumbs on his shirt and realized that he looked like he might have put on a pound or two. *'Poor Adam. He'll never keep it off,'* she thought. He looked over at her at that moment and she smiled at him, hoping it would mask her thoughts.

Nick sat down at the other end of the table, distracting her. "All right then," he began. "Let's put this whole thing together." He looked at Samantha. "Let's begin with you, Ms. Sanders. Tell us what happened on the night that your husband was killed."

Samantha sighed. Better to get this over with as quickly as possible. "I went to the museum with Jeremy. He'd been asked by Dulcie to be a part of the events that night. We mingled around then went up to the boardroom. He did his thing with the wine," Dulcie noticed the annoyance creeping into Samantha's voice when she said this, "then afterward, *he*," she gestured at Patrick, "thought he could just walk up and start talking with me like nothing had ever happened." Her face had twisted into a look of disgust.

"Note for the record that the witness is pointing to Patrick Spratt," Johnson said quietly in the direction of the voice recorder. They had all been told it was being used, but Samantha started when Johnson spoke.

"What do you mean, 'witness'?" she asked warily.

"You may all be called as witnesses in Brendan MacArthur's trial," Nick said.

"You mean this isn't the end of it?" Samantha squeaked.

"Perhaps not, although it could be if you aren't needed for trial," Nick answered.

Samantha sat back in her chair and took a deep breath.

"You okay?" Dulcie asked quietly.

Samantha nodded.

"Can you continue? What happened after Mr. Spratt spoke with you?" Nick prompted.

Samantha stared at the table. "First, I yelled at *Mr. Patrick Spratt*," she enunciated his name, "and told him to get away from me. Then his uncle, *Mr. Geoffrey Spratt*, insulted me with his comments. Everyone cleared out of the room, and I got mad at Jeremy. He hadn't even tried to defend me!" Samantha was shaking now and looked as though she was about to burst into tears. "I stormed out and went downstairs. Jeremy came down and got me in a cab. Alone. I went home. He stayed. He said there were people there who could help his career." Samantha suddenly looked up, her head whipping back and forth, eyeing everyone at the table. "What about *my* career? What about the years that I'd been the stupid Weather Girl?" she ranted.

Dulcie and Nick exchanged glances. Neither dared correct her with 'weather *forecaster*' at the moment.

"I just went home and fell asleep after that," Samantha continued. "When I woke up in the morning, Jeremy wasn't home. It wasn't unusual. But then I called around and couldn't find him. Then you guys arrived," she pointed to Nick and Johnson.

"Witness is indicating detectives Nicholas Black and Adam Johnson," Johnson said quietly.

The room was silent for a moment. They all looked at Nick. "Mr. Patrick Spratt, could you tell us your movements that night," Nick said.

Patrick looked very pale. Recent events had been sobering. He had never seen the inside of a holding cell before and didn't want to again anytime soon.

"My uncle picked me up from my apartment right around the time the event was starting. We went to the museum, had some champagne, then went up to the boardroom. After the tasting I did try to talk to Sam, but as you've heard already, that didn't work out. Uncle Geoffrey took me home. I stayed up for a few hours basically contemplating my life, then I went to bed." Patrick was very concise. He didn't mention watching the video of Samantha on television for most of the night.

"Thank you," Nick said. "Now we come to Mr. Geoffrey Spratt," he said.

Geoffrey looked indignant. "Look, you already have a confession from the guy. Why are we all here, anyway? I'm sure you don't really need any of us as witnesses. I think I should have a lawyer present," he concluded.

Nick was ready for him. "All of you are, of course, speaking voluntarily right now. We're simply trying to clarify the facts so that we can conclude this case as quickly as possible. In that light, however, I might point out that your refusal to speak may extend this investigation which I don't think any of us wants."

The others mumbled their agreement.

"Fine," Geoffrey sputtered. "I did everything that Patrick just said. After I dropped him off, I went home and then to bed. That's it."

"There, that wasn't too hard," Johnson whispered facetiously. Only Dulcie heard him. She looked down at her lap to hide her smile.

"Now we come to motivations," Nick said. "Each of you had reason to end the life of Jeremy Plunkett," he stated. "We have evidence to suggest that. Samantha Sanders stands to receive a sizeable life insurance policy," he began.

A gasp came from Samantha. "How did you know that?" she wailed.

"The insurance company contacted the police since the death was suspicious," Johnsons said. "Standard procedure. By the way, when are you due?" he asked.

"I.. well… the baby…," Samantha stammered.

"What?" Patrick now sputtered. "A baby?" He turned to his uncle. "Look, I wanted her back for sure. But I do *not* want to bring up someone else's brat!" he hissed.

"Look, she's just pregnant. The kid might not even happen. Or it could get adopted," Geoffrey said before he could stop himself.

The others now stared at him, aghast. "What I mean to say is…," he began.

"What you mean to say is that you are a conniving, scheming bastard! I've been thanking my lucky stars every day that I didn't marry your loser of a nephew!" she shouted.

Geoffrey looked disgusted. "Yeah, how are you gonna raise a kid on your own? It isn't like you have money. And I'm sure the TV station doesn't want a pregnant weather girl," he barked.

Samantha's eyes riveted on Geoffrey Spratt. "Let me clarify a few matters for you, you spiteful little troll," she said menacingly. "First, Jeremy left me well provided for." She put her hand on her stomach as if to protect the baby. Johnson saw the gesture and looked at Nick as if to say, "told you so!"

"Second," Samantha continued, "a pregnant woman on television is not the pariah that it was during the Dark Ages when you were raised. And third, I am a weather *forecaster*, otherwise known as a meteorologist, a professional title. I am *not* a weather *girl*."

Nick and Dulcie tried not to look at each other. They knew that they would both grin if they did. Dulcie had also decided not to bring up the fact that Samantha had just contradicted her previous outburst about her profession.

Geoffrey grunted and looked away.

Samantha managed to collect herself. She sat up straight in a businesslike fashion. "Here's the part that I don't understand," she said. "Why did Brendan put the other wine in that bottle anyway? Didn't he know that he wouldn't fool Jeremy?" she asked.

"What?!" Geoffrey now squawked.

Nick chuckled. "Oh that's right! You haven't heard," he said, turning to Geoffrey. "The 1869 Château Lafite Rothschild is pretty much worthless. Brendan knew that from the start. He was trying to pass off a more recent version as the 1869 so that he could sell it all in perhaps a clandestine manner." Nick's gaze riveted on Geoffrey.

The man turned purple. "I have to make a call," he said quickly, his chair scraping on the floor as he stood.

"Sit down," Johnson quietly ordered. "That's all been taken care of."

Geoffrey looked over at him, bewildered. "What do you… I don't know what you mean," he said.

"Your deposit into a certain account in the Cayman Islands has not gone through. Brendan MacArthur's bank accounts were frozen as soon as he was arrested. He had a number of them around the world. Interpol had taken notice, you see," Nick said. "You're a very lucky man," he added.

Geoffrey's knees collapsed under him and he crumpled into his chair.

"Of course we could still arrest you for conspiring to purchase archeological finds that belong to the government," Nick said.

"But how was I to know where it came from?" Geoffrey whined in his defense.

"Shut it," Johnson ordered. "You're fortunate. The sale didn't go through so there are no charges. We would advise you to be more careful with your investments in the future, however."

Patrick patted his uncle on the shoulder. Geoffrey jerked away. "No thanks to you for any of this," he sneered at him.

Nick collected the notes in front of him and rose from his seat abruptly. "Well, I think this concludes our investigation. Thank you all for coming. Johnson will see you out," he said. He left the room.

Johnson clicked off the voice recorder and motioned to Geoffrey, Patrick, and Samantha.

"Could you tell me where the restroom is please?" Samantha said. She looked decidedly green.

"Follow me," Dulcie interjected. They quickly made their way down the hall. Dulcie held open the door as Samantha rushed in and directly into a stall. Several moments later she joined Dulcie at the row of sinks.

"You okay?" Dulcie asked.

Samantha splashed water on her face and rinsed out her mouth. Dulcie handed her a paper towel.

"I'm sorry. It isn't pretty," Samantha said. "They make pregnancy sound all nice and rosy, but in reality it's pretty awful."

Dulcie nodded. "Seems like it," she said. "Samantha, are you regretting this? I mean, are you unhappy about having a baby?"

Samantha looked thoughtful. She opened her purse and found a hairbrush. "Not unhappy," she said, fixing her hair. "I think I'm more apprehensive." She stopped and turned to Dulcie. "To be honest, I'm actually glad to have the excuse to leave that job. I mean, it isn't that I'm pregnant. That's not why I'm going to leave it. It's the fact that my husband was killed. I'd always be 'That-Weather-Girl-Whose-Husband-Was-Murdered'. No one would be able to get beyond that. Add that to my being pregnant and…"

"I'm sure ratings would go up," Dulcie laughed.

"Sad commentary on the world in general," Samantha replied. "No, I think that I'll go back to school, finish my doctorate and go into research like I'd always planned. I'll have some money, so I'll be able to do all of that and take good care of Junior here, too," she said, rubbing her belly.

"I'm glad to hear it," Dulcie said. "I do have a question though, and I didn't want to bring it up earlier," she said. "During my last encounter with Brendan, he said something about you 'suggesting' that Patrick had killed your husband. What was that all about?"

"Oh," said Samantha. She busied herself putting away her brush. A guilty looked had crossed her face.

Dulcie was silent. Finally Samantha looked back up at her. "I met with Brendan. I wanted to plant the seed that Patrick had done it. I was furious at Patrick and his uncle. But it wasn't as bad is that. You see, I really did think that Patrick had killed Jeremy. Patrick had been stalking me, and I thought he'd taken things to the next step, so…" she said, not finishing the sentence.

"And you were not only furious, but scared," Dulcie said, completing the thought. "I can see that.

Probably not the best way to go about things, but then you were in a tough situation."

"I'm not proud of it, certainly," Samantha added. "I'm just glad to have all of this over."

"Me too," Dulcie agreed.

❦

Dulcie stood in the gallery of the Little Ice Age exhibit looking intently at *The Magpie*. An insurance adjuster stood beside her. They both watched a highly paid artwork restorer carefully examining the painting with a magnifying glass. "You're in luck, I believe," she said at last. "I can only find a tiny knick that the keys made. It's up to the museum that owns the work whether or not they want it repaired."

The adjustor looked relieved. "I'll contact them with the news. Perhaps they'll accept it as is. The incident does add an interesting chapter to the provenance, after all," he remarked. "How many people throw a set of keys at an invaluable Monet to set off an alarm and save their own lives?" He shook his head in disbelief, then stepped away from her and took out his cell phone.

"How many, indeed?" A quiet voice behind Dulcie said. She turned to face her brother. "Got yourself out of another scrape, I see," he said. "Gee, Dulcie. You go from dating a criminal to dating a cop. At least your taste in men is improving."

She smacked him on the arm but then said ruefully, "I'm not sure which is easier to handle."

"Oh, I think you know," he countered. "Nick's a pretty great guy."

"Yeah, he is," Dulcie agreed.

"So…," Dan prompted. He began whistling Mendelssohn's 'Wedding March'.

Dulcie turned on her heel and began walking away.

"Hey, you could do worse!" Dan called out to her. "In fact, you have!"

Dulcie kept walking, but Dan knew his sister. She'd barely make it back to her office before she started laughing.

The Dulcie Chambers Museum Mysteries

Book #1
An Exhibit of Madness
(Previously titled: Portrait of a Murder)

Dr. Dulcinea ("Dulcie") Chambers has a lot on her mind. She's just opened a new exhibit of Winslow Homer watercolors at the Maine Museum of Art where she's Chief Curator. The exhibit will be complete when the museum's director, the urbane Joshua Harriman, buys the final piece at auction. But when Dulcie discovers a body where the painting should have been, she's one of the primary suspects. Portland Police Detective Nicholas Black is on the case but finds he is less than objective when it comes to the attractive Dr. Chambers.

Book #2
From the Murky Deep

Detective Nicholas Black has cause for concern. He's investigating the suspicious death of a young woman whose body has just washed on shore in full scuba gear. Normally it would simply be a case of drowning, yet along with this particular body is a stolen Vincent van Gogh painting in a watertight tube. To further complicate matters, the phone number of Dr. Dulcinea (Dulcie) Chambers is written on the dead woman's hand. As the new director of the Maine

Museum of Art, Dulcie is already busy negotiating the sale of one of the museum's pieces with a wealthy collector. When Dulcie learns that she's a chief suspect however, she has no choice but to help with the investigation. Dulcie finds herself diving in to solve this mystery as her relationship with Detective Nicholas Black also reaches new depths.

BOOK #3
THE FRAGILE FLOWER

World-renowned abstract expressionist painter Logan Dumbarton is welcomed to the Maine Museum of Art to teach a master class to a group of talented local artists. But he proves more difficult than any of the staff, along with his stunning yet whiny wife and his spinster/business-manager sister, can handle with his constant complaints and egocentric demeanor. Within a week the entire class loathes him. Is he really worth all this trouble? Somebody doesn't seem to think so and it's up to Dr. Dulcinea ("Dulcie") Chambers to find out who. But she'll have to team up with Detective Nicholas Black once again, and their relationship at the moment can only be described as *fragile*.

BOOK #4
A MIND WITHIN

While assembling a new exhibit featuring *Art Brut* or "Outsider Art," Dr. Dulcinea ("Dulcie") Chambers encounters an enormously talented and equally troubled young man, Xander Bellamy. An autistic savant, Xander has not communicated with anyone for several months, since his father was sent to prison for the murder of Xander's domineering grandfather. Detective Nicholas Black thought the case was closed until Dulcie came to him with compelling evidence that the real killer was still at large. When evidence had originally pointed to Xander as the murderer, Xander's father had quickly confessed. Did he do this to save his son from being committed to a mental institution for the criminally insane? Xander's battle-axe aunt has come to live with him and, along with long-time family housekeeper Giselle, they see to his needs. But is there more to them than meets the eye? Meanwhile Dulcie seeks to see inside Xander's mind with the help of psychologist Dr. Raymond Armand. However, the ambitious Armand has other ideas about the lovely Dr. Chambers and is about to give Nicholas Black some competition when it comes to her affections.

If you would like to read the Dulcie Chambers Museum Mysteries please visit the author's website (kerryjcharles.com) for more information or request copies at your local bookstore or library. Ebook versions are also available from major suppliers online.

Reviews from thoughtful readers are always welcome on any website or media outlet. Thank you!

ABOUT THE AUTHOR

Kerry J Charles has worked as a researcher, writer, and editor for *National Geographic*, the Smithsonian Institution, Harvard University and several major textbook publishers. She holds four degrees including a Masters in Geospatial Engineering and a Masters in Art History from Harvard University. She has carried out research in many of the world's art museums as a freelance writer and scholar.

A swimmer, scuba diver, golfer, and boating enthusiast, Charles enjoys seeing the world from above and below sea level as well as from the tee box. Her life experiences inspire her writing and she is always seeking out new travels and adventures. She returned to her roots in coastal Maine while writing the Dulcie Chambers Museum Mysteries.

Printed in the USA
CPSIA information can be obtained
at www.ICGtesting.com
LVHW042331230524
781273LV00032B/303